"Some things are inevitable, Willa."

Clay whispered the words as his mouth continued to move enticingly across hers. "You can fight them only so long."

"But we can't," she pleaded softly as she felt Clay's lips brush hers in a feather-light kiss. With each caressing stroke of his mouth, something wild was ignited within her, something that demanded fulfillment no matter what the cost. Suddenly terrified, she managed to evade his lips. "We have to stop. Please, Clay."

"Maybe we are rushing things." Clay's hands lingered at her waist.

Willa shook her head. "This shouldn't be happening between us at all, Clay. It can't." *Besides, there's no real trust between us. And there never can be,* her heart added silently.

Susan Fox is an American writer living in Des Moines, Iowa, where she was born. She is married and has two sons, and is happy now to add to her occupation as ''housewife'' that of author. Her enjoyment in reading romances led to writing them and reflects an early interest in westerns and cowboys. She won a Romance Writers of America Golden Heart Award in 1984 and 1985.

Books by Susan Fox

HARLEQUIN ROMANCE
2763—VOWS OF THE HEART

Don't miss any of our special offers. Write to us at the following address for information on our newest releases.

Harlequin Reader Service
901 Fuhrmann Blvd., P.O. Box 1397, Buffalo, NY 14240
Canadian address: P.O. Box 603,
Fort Erie, Ont. L2A 5X3

The Black
Sheep
Susan Fox

Harlequin Books

TORONTO • NEW YORK • LONDON
AMSTERDAM • PARIS • SYDNEY • HAMBURG
STOCKHOLM • ATHENS • TOKYO • MILAN

ISBN 0-373-02930-6

Harlequin Romance first edition September 1988

CHAPTER ONE

WILLA ROSS walked up the grassy incline, silently taking a spot just off to the side of the large group of mourners who had gathered for the graveside service. She didn't join her Aunt Tess and her cousin, Paige, the only ones seated beneath the emerald canopy that shaded the flower-draped casket; her estrangement from them and her late uncle, Calvin Harding, had been too traumatic and had lasted too long for her to believe she would have been welcome there.

So she remained where she was, the small ridge of sod she was standing on affording her a clear view of the minister and what remained of her family, her position there also making it easier for her to slip away later unnoticed.

From where he stood with the other pallbearers, Clayton Cantrell's dark gaze veered toward the movement at the edge of the crowd, catching sight of Willa the moment she stopped a few feet short of the other mourners. A shock wave of rage and grief rolled over him and settled like a rock in his middle as recognition pounded through him.

Slim, clad in a simple fawn-colored dress he suspected was a subtle indication that she didn't mourn too deeply for her Uncle Cal, Willa Ross looked little different from the mischievous minx she'd been as a teenager. Though her sandy-brown hair had been twisted into a prim knot that suggested maturity, her features were much the same delicate, pretty ones they'd been at seventeen. Five years had only enhanced the beauty she'd had back then.

The weight inside him began to twist. It was because of Willa Ross that his kid sister, Angela, had been denied the same chance to mature or grow to womanhood. Because of Willa Ross, little Angie lay just over the hill in a grave next to their parents'.

The bitterness he thought had eased over the years suddenly filled his heart and deepened the harsh grooves that bracketed his mouth.

"Shall we recite the Lord's Prayer?" the minister suggested, then bowed his head as he began, "'Our Father, Who art in Heaven...'"

Willa didn't bow her head as everyone else did, taking the opportunity as she repeated the words of the prayer softly to study her aunt. The past five years hadn't been kind to her Aunt Tess. Willa's green eyes welled with tears as she noted how frail and sickly the woman looked, her complexion lined and chalky, her hair shot through with gray. Aunt Tess's small hands were slightly gnarled now and lay trembling in a desolate clasp in her lap.

Willa would have given anything to be the one at her aunt's side, the one who consoled and offered strength, the one to share her sorrow. But Willa was the family outcast, unsure even now just how welcome her presence would be. She had been unable to stay away from this service, prepared to be satisfied with only a distant glimpse of the woman who'd raised her after her parents' deaths, yet miserable with the secret, gut-wrenching hope that the horrible rift between them could somehow miraculously be healed now that her Uncle Cal was dead.

"'And forgive us our sins as we forgive those who sin against us...'"

Clay Cantrell repeated the words by rote, without thought to their meaning, his hard black eyes fixed on Willa's face, callous to the heartsick curve of her soft mouth and the aura of melancholia about her.

As if Willa sensed his hostility, her gaze suddenly swung, then impacted with his.

Black eyes cold with dislike caused the words of the prayer to lodge in her throat. Abruptly silenced, Willa couldn't look away from that tanned, ruggedly handsome face with its strong, well-constructed contours and bold male cut of mouth, couldn't resist letting her eyes make a quick assessment of the tall, wide-shouldered, lean-hipped body that was nearly a foot taller than her own. Dark-haired, dressed entirely in black, from the Stetson he held in his hand to his suit and dress boots, Clay Cantrell was a towering, intimidating man—almost frightening—and nothing like the tolerant, indulgent older brother of her best friend she'd known him to be so long ago.

"Amen." The minister concluded the recitation, then led the mourners in a verse from what she recognized was one of Aunt Tess's favorite hymns. As Willa forced herself to focus on her aunt and avoid looking Clay's way again, she mouthed the words of the hymn, her chest suddenly too tight with pain for any sound to come out.

Coming here had been a mistake. One glimpse of Clay Cantrell's grim expression had convinced her of that.

It was at just the moment the minister began to make a few last remarks about Calvin Harding's passing that Aunt Tess turned her head and let her pained gaze sweep over the crowd. Taken by surprise, Willa didn't move those first few seconds. And then it was too late.

Tess Harding's glance connected with Willa's, and for a stunned moment, neither could react. Then, as if suddenly oblivious to the concluding service, Tess got unsteadily to her feet. A ripple of surprise rustled through the crowd as Tess laid her handbag on her chair. The minister hesitated, then hastily finished his last sentence, a frown of concern on his face as Tess started to walk away. Paige rose from her chair, clearly startled by her mother's behavior.

Willa felt as if she'd turned to stone, sick with apprehension as her aunt headed grimly toward her. By then, everyone else was turning to see who or what it was Tess was staring at so intently. All sound and movement halted as Willa was recognized.

It took every bit of strength Willa had just to stand there, teetering on the razor's edge of taut nerves as she waited for her aunt's rejection or acceptance. She had the horrifying sensation that the woman coming toward her so determinedly was someone she didn't know at all, and she tried valiantly to steel herself against certain rejection.

And then Tess's grim expression eased. Hope surged in Willa's heart as Tess's mouth curved into a watery smile. Just as Willa started forward to grasp her aunt's outstretched hands, Tess suddenly faltered, stopped, then collapsed onto the grass.

For the first few seconds no one but Willa moved; it was as if no one could believe his eyes. Distantly

Willa heard her cousin shriek as she fell to her knees and searched at her aunt's wrist for a pulse. Terror beat a sickening cadence in her chest as she detected nothing. And then the chaos began.

"Someone get my medical bag!" Dr. Elliot came rushing over, then crouched to gently move Tess onto her back. The minister bustled to Willa's side and helped her to her feet. She watched helplessly as the doctor felt for a pulse, relieved when he appeared to find it. Already his station wagon was being driven off the cemetery lane toward them while one of the mourners came running ahead with his medical bag. In seconds he was alternately listening with his stethoscope and issuing orders.

Willa was startled by a strident feminine indictment.

"This is your fault."

Willa turned dazed eyes toward her cousin, Paige.

"Why did you have to show up?" the brunette demanded. "My God, if she dies..."

Clay Cantrell was at Paige's side instantly, his arm going around her consolingly.

"If she dies—" Paige repeated tremulously, unable to voice the threat as she turned her face and pressed it against Clay's chest, her heartrending sobs racking her slim frame and causing Clay to wrap her more tightly in his arms.

Over Paige's perfectly coiffed head, Clay's dark eyes were livid with accusation as they bore down on Willa. He quickly surveyed the large crowd of mourners comprised of ranching neighbors and townspeople. Their expressions echoed both the sympathy felt toward Paige and the harsh reproach directed toward Willa.

"I think you'd better clear out." Clay's deep voice rumbled threateningly and a muscle worked at his jaw.

Willa cast a worried glance at her aunt first, then was forced to step a little out of the way as a couple of men lifted a portable stretcher from the back of the doctor's station wagon.

"Please, Clay, make her go." Paige's plea was partly muffled against the lapel of Clay's suit jacket.

"Willa?" Clay's voice was a chilling menace.

Daring to hesitate, Willa tore her eyes from the warning in Clay's. "Will she be all right?" she asked the doctor as her aunt was lifted onto the stretcher.

"Don't know," he answered gruffly as he waited for the stretcher to be loaded into the back of his car. Willa was dismissed with a curt turn of his head. "Would you like to ride along, Paige?" the doctor asked her cousin solicitously.

Willa stepped back as Dr. Elliot brushed past her to escort Paige to the front passenger seat of the car. In moments, the doctor was in the back with his patient, while a volunteer drove the big vehicle over the un- broken sod to the lane, then on toward the highway and town.

Wanting to follow, Willa hurried across the grass toward where she had double-parked her car earlier. She had almost reached it, when she heard the long stride of booted feet behind her. Sensing instantly who it was, she tried to increase her pace, but steellike fin- gers caught her arm and swung her roughly around.

Wary green eyes flew upward to meet the black in- tensity of Clay's, not surprised by the flat, unfriendly depths.

"What the hell are you doing here?"

Willa tried to pull out of his grip but couldn't. "Paying my last respects," she answered, her voice bearing the faintest hint of insolence.

And that insolence riled him. Clay released her arm, aware that the dark feelings she aroused made him capable of bruising her.

"The funeral's over, so you can move on," he advised.

"I'm going to the hospital," she said, her slim body rigid with defiance.

"No one wants you there."

Clay felt something inside him soften at the anguish that flickered over her face before she could mask it. That Willa had suffered these past years was apparent to him, now that he could see the haunting evidence of it in her eyes.

But suffering and sadness were things he didn't want to see, changes he didn't want to acknowledge. This girl's actions had taken his sister's life and he'd be damned if he'd let himself feel sorry for her.

"Go back to wherever it is you came from. There's nothing for you here," he said, the harshness in his voice a denial of the compassion that had tugged at him those few moments.

"I want to make certain Aunt Tess is all right."

"I think you've done enough."

Clay's words robbed her of breath as his implication hit her squarely in the chest. *He blamed her for this, too.* The realization was staggering, but somehow she managed to withstand the pain and return his condemning stare. It was hard to believe that this man's affection for his sister had once extended to her.

Willa turned and walked the last steps to the car. She was just about to reach for the door handle, when Clay reached around her and opened it for her.

"Don't go to the hospital, Willa. You'll just upset everyone again and stir up the past."

"Maybe it needs to be stirred up," she challenged quietly, turning her head to look up at his iron expression.

"She's a sick woman, Willa. If you want another death on your conscience, then go on over to that hospital," he prodded, and Willa's face went ashen.

Without another word, she got into her car, not even looking Clay's way when he closed the door beside her. Fumbling in her purse for the key, she jammed it into the ignition and gave it a twist. As she drove away, she cast a last glance in the rearview mirror at the tall dark-haired man dressed in black who watched her go.

WILLA STEPPED OUT of the service station rest room, changed from her dress, stockings and heels into a plaid shirt, jeans and her well-worn western boots. Her dark blond hair had been released from confinement and tumbled freely just past her shoulders.

She went directly to her car, passing up a last opportunity for a quick meal at the truck-stop diner next door. She wasn't fit to be seen after the storm of heartbroken tears that had left her eyes puffy and red with bruiselike shadows beneath them. The few cosmetics she carried in her purse had covered over some of the evidence, but not enough for her to feel comfortable in public.

She quickly tossed her things into the small suitcase in the trunk. Next to it, the larger case she'd filled with enough clothes to last a week mocked her. She'd had such hope when she'd packed it. Now she knew those hopes were gone. There was truly no going back. Even if she could, there would be no way to expose the horrible lies of the past without further jeopardizing her aunt's health. Judging from the hostility shown her by everyone at the funeral, no one would believe her now any more than they had then. The realization depressed her.

She'd not gone to the hospital, after all, too frightened that Clay was right. She couldn't bear to have another life on her conscience. Feeling responsible for her best friend's death when they were both seventeen was bad enough.

Willa slammed the trunk closed the instant the old memory stirred, determined to keep it suppressed. She'd learned never to let it totally surface, though it often haunted her dreams and made her nights long, restless ordeals.

The late-model car started easily, as it always did, and Willa slipped it into gear, heading out of the gas station for the interstate to continue her long drive home. She was still only about fifty miles from Cascade. Fifty miles from her real home, came the thought before Willa pushed it away.

These days, home was the D & R, a little ranch over two hundred miles from Cascade, Wyoming, just northeast of Colorado Springs, Colorado, and had been for the past three years. She was part-owner of a modest ranch where she and her partner, Ivy Dayton, raised quarter horses. Willa ran the ranch and helped train the horses, while Ivy saw to their breeding and took them to horse shows. Willa had sunk a major portion of the money she'd inherited from her parents into her half of the ranch. It had been a prosperous investment for her, and one that had demanded long, tiring hours—just what Willa had needed—until Ivy sent word from a horse show in Wyoming that she'd read Calvin Harding's obituary. Willa knew she had to attend at least some part of his funeral.

It was Uncle Cal who had banished Willa from their home the day she turned eighteen, warning her never to come back. Although Aunt Tess had tearfully begged him to reconsider, in the end she had submitted to his edict. Willa had been on her own from then on.

Remembering Tess's reluctance to throw her out had inspired the crazy idea that perhaps she and her aunt could be reconciled now that her uncle was no longer alive to prevent it. She knew now that it just wasn't to be.

At the next interchange, a state patrol car came down the ramp, merging into the lane a few car lengths behind her. Willa automatically glanced at her speedometer and continued on, confident she was obeying the speed limit.

Startled by the patrol car's siren a few moments later, she checked her rearview mirror to see the cruiser bearing down on her, red lights flashing. Willa pulled onto the shoulder as quickly and safely as possible, fully expecting the patrolman to drive on past since she hadn't been violating any traffic law. To her surprise, he pulled up behind her, then got out of his car to approach hers.

Tension knotted painfully in her stomach as she recalled the other time she'd had to deal with a lawman. She'd never got over it. To this day she felt intimidated by police officers, frightened to attract their attention in any way, frightened that her word wouldn't be believed and she'd again be subjected to another traumatic questioning.

Seeing the patrolman beside the car, Willa hastily rolled down her window.

"Evening, miss. Would your name happen to be Willa Ross?"

Though the patrolman was a model of courtesy and respect, Willa felt a sharp tingle of apprehension. She nodded.

"Well, Miss Ross, I'm sorry to relate to you that it seems you have a family emergency back in Cascade. They've requested that we try to locate you and provide you with an escort back as soon as possible."

Willa's chest went tight. Suddenly she feared the worst. "Do you know any of the details?" she got out around a tongue thick with emotion. Her aunt had died; she just knew it.

The patrolman shook his head. "No, miss, I'm afraid I don't, but I was under the impression they were in a big hurry for you to get back there. Thought you might have been across the state line by now. Lucky you aren't, since it'll take that much less time for you to get back."

Willa was having a difficult time keeping back her tears. If the patrolman felt there was reason to hurry, it might mean her aunt was still alive. The request for Willa's presence would have had to be her aunt's idea—and one Paige would never have stood for unless it had been a deathbed request.

"Are you all right, miss?"

"I'll be all right," she assured the officer.

"You sure?" The patrolman's concern for her was genuine, and she felt herself relax. She could see compassion in his warm brown gaze and wondered why the sheriff who'd confronted her five years earlier hadn't possessed even an ounce of this officer's humanity.

"I'll be fine. You mentioned an escort?"

"That I did," he said with a smile, which she found herself returning. "If you'll follow me, Miss Ross, we'll get started."

They were back on the interstate in moments and, after making use of a turnaround for emergency vehicles, they were headed north toward Cascade.

"Thank you so much, Officer," Willa said once they'd reached the hospital and she got out of her car. The patrolman had left his cruiser idling just a few feet away to come over and speak to her.

"My pleasure, Miss Ross," he returned with a smile. "Good luck." Willa nodded her acceptance, then hurried on in to the emergency entrance. Discovering that her aunt had been taken to the cardiac care unit, she went directly to the elevators.

She'd pressed the button for the third floor before she allowed herself to again consider why her "family" had asked the highway patrol to summon her back to Cascade. Her aunt was evidently not expected to live. A crush of guilt came down on her. If she'd not attended the funeral and given her aunt a shock, Tess wouldn't be lying in the CCU about to die. Willa looked down at her clenched hands. She didn't know how she could bear the responsibility for a death a second time.

The elevator doors slid open and Willa stepped out, going directly to the nurses' station, where she was directed to the wing that housed the CCU. Willa did her best to harden herself to the reception she knew was waiting, realizing the moment she stepped into the crowded waiting room that she wouldn't have the strength to develop that kind of hard veneer. The most she could manage was to mask her feelings and project the illusion of toughness.

It was one of her aunt's closest friends, Mabel Asner, who first saw her and announced, "Well, now, here's Willa Ross." The small, plump woman fixed a critical eye on Willa's blue plaid shirt and jeans. The quiet conversations in the small room ceased. There wasn't a face in the room that offered any kind of welcome, and more than one gaze went directly to Clay Cantrell, as if to gauge his reaction to her arrival.

Clay's flinty expression revealed nothing as he stood leaning against the far wall, his suit coat, tie and vest discarded, his crisp white shirt partially unbuttoned. Diamond-hard eyes went over Willa from head to toe, their cold scrutiny sending a chill through her.

Next to him Paige sat staring at her accusingly, and Willa felt the old anger rise and swell. The enmity between the two cousins was too strong to go undetected. There wasn't a person in the small room who didn't feel it—or misjudge its reason. As it always had been, Paige was everyone's darling, her long jet hair, violet eyes and satiny perfect skin enchanting them all. Unfortunately the high regard everyone had for Tess caused them to believe Paige possessed the same fine qualities of gentleness and good character her mother did. Few other than Willa and Paige herself knew the truth of that.

Willa took a quick breath and started across the room to her cousin. "How is she?" Willa asked, already knowing what kind of response her question would get.

"Dr. Elliot says she's stabilized. No thanks to you," Paige added.

"I'm surprised you went to all the trouble of having the state patrol track me down."

Paige's eyes were half-lidded with contempt. "Mother was asking for you. The doctor thought it wise to cater to her, or you wouldn't be here. I wouldn't have let you get within a hundred miles of her a second time," Paige vowed, and by the whispering that went on in the room behind Willa she knew most felt the same way. Tess was a well-liked woman, and in view of the recent death of her husband, her friends would naturally feel very protective of her. Willa felt hurt that anyone would think her aunt had to be protected from her.

"When can I see her?"

"If she doesn't mention you when she wakes up again, then never."

Willa felt her face go bloodless. It was no less than she should have expected. Perhaps the delicate lines of strain on her cousin's lovely face were there more out of fear for herself than grief for her late father or worry for her mother's life. Only Willa knew what secrets Paige concealed beneath the cruelty and scorn she showed her. She could easily imagine Paige's eagerness to have her out of their lives again and away from Cascade forever.

"Paige." Dr. Elliot stood in the doorway, beckoning her into the privacy of the hall. Paige rose gracefully and glanced back beseechingly at Clay, who then escorted her out. Willa was left standing awkwardly in the waiting room, staring after them. Anxiously she watched for any sign that the doctor was delivering bad news, relieved when Paige's face darkened in anger rather than agony.

"You'd better step out here, too," the doctor called to Willa from the hall, the stern way he looked and spoke to her making his disapproval evident.

Willa hurried to comply, her heart racing. Just as she reached the small group, Paige made a little sound of despair, then pulled her arm from Clay's to rush down the hall to the nearest rest room. Mabel Asner rose immediately to go after Paige and offer consolation. And probably, Willa thought unkindly, to be the first to glean whatever grist for gossip she could.

"You can step in for five minutes, Willa, not a moment more," Doc Elliot cautioned, then warned, "She can't take any kind of upset right now, so don't you give her any."

"I wouldn't," Willa said, stung at his tone.

"Your presence alone might do it," he pronounced. "If it even looks like this is too much for her, I want you out of there. I won't care how much Tess says she wants to see you, I'll forbid it. Understand?"

Willa's cheeks reddened. She was outraged at being spoken to in such a manner. Her green eyes were flashing. "I understand completely." She clenched her teeth on a more scathing retort, mindful of the fact that she had another chance with her aunt because it was this man's professional opinion that Tess ought to have her wish.

"All right," he said reluctantly, watching her closely. "Tell one of the nurses outside the unit who you are before you go in."

Willa turned and walked toward the end of the corridor to the short hall that led to the CCU. She tried to ignore the booted steps that shadowed hers as Clay fell in beside her. He didn't say a word to her until she stopped to speak to the nurse.

"I'll be watching, Willa."

Willa's eyes flew to his, his quiet warning telling her plainly just how great the chasm of hostility and mistrust between them was.

"You do that, Clay," she murmured as he took a position in front of the observation window, his masculine stance bearing the cold, unrelenting arrogance of an enemy.

CHAPTER TWO

WILLA ENTERED the cardiac unit, hesitating just inside the door as the enormity of it all struck her. Aunt Tess was lying in one of four beds, and Willa's heart ached at the number of wires and tubes connected to her frail body. The constant click, whir and blip of the life-monitoring equipment in the room emphasized how gravely ill each patient was. As she approached Tess's bed, she was suddenly terrified that her visit would be too much for her aunt.

Willa glanced back anxiously at the nurse who had accompanied her and who was now standing at the foot of Tess's bed. The nurse nodded her encouragement and Willa reached out hesitantly to touch her aunt's thin hand.

"I'm here, Aunt Tess."

Tess's eyes fluttered a moment before opening fully and finding Willa.

"Willa." Tess mouthed her name more than spoke it, clearly weak. Her dove-gray eyes were soft, and her pale lips twitched with the extra effort it took to smile. Willa's heart was wrung mercilessly and she gently pressed her aunt's hand between both of hers. "Missed you so," she whispered, and Willa felt the sharp sting of tears.

"I've missed you, too, Auntie." Willa's voice wobbled as she rubbed the back of her aunt's hand.

"Please...stay," Tess said. "I want you with me."

"I will," Willa vowed, distressed when her aunt's eyes fell shut. She was willing to promise her anything if it would keep her alive and make her well.

Tess opened her eyes again. "Kept your room...just the way it was." She blinked as if her eyelids were heavy weights, then appeared to rest a moment. "I want you to come home."

Willa's eyes clogged with more tears. Going back to the Circle H ranch was impossible now, but there was no reason for her aunt to know that just yet. Since she and Tess had had no contact with each other the past five years, Tess didn't know about the life she'd made for herself in Colorado.

The nurse stepped forward and touched Willa's shoulder, signaling her it was time to leave. It was obvious Tess was already too spent to talk longer.

"I have to leave now, Aunt Tess," Willa said, leaning down to kiss her aunt's cheek. "Get a good night's rest. I'll be back in the morning."

Tess's eyes closed a last time and she drifted off into exhausted slumber. Willa tenderly released her hand and backed away from the bed. She was shaking and her eyes were blurred as she followed the nurse from the unit.

"A lot of it's the medication she's on," the nurse explained reassuringly when she saw Willa's flushed face.

"Will she live?" Willa had to ask the question.

"She's stable. The next forty-eight hours will tell." The nurse glanced back at Tess. "She was sure determined to see you."

Willa was too emotional to respond to the nurse's comment or linger. She hurriedly stepped into the hall as the tears began. Unfortunately Clay was still waiting, and she made a swift effort to control herself. What she felt was too deep and too personal to be witnessed by a man who held such ill will toward her.

"What did she say?"

"I'm surprised you don't read lips," Willa hedged as she started to walk away from him. Blindly she fumbled through her purse for Kleenex, hoping to stem the fountain of threatening tears by blowing her nose. She stopped just before she reached the doorway into the main hall, unable to suppress a sob of frustration when she discovered that all she had left was a single shredded tissue.

"Here." Clay's gruff voice drew her attention to the spotless white handkerchief he pressed into her fingers.

"Thanks." Willa turned away from him, her back rigid. She used the hankie to muffle her sudden attack of sniffles.

Clay watched, detecting the tremors that went through her small body, irritated that he couldn't be indifferent to her feelings. But, then, something about Willa had always affected him, even when she'd been a child. Clay's mouth formed a bitter line as his dark gaze wandered down her slim back to her shapely backside and her jeans-clad legs. Something else about Willa was affecting him now, and he was damn sure he wanted no part of it.

Willa quickly blotted her eyes, acutely aware of Clay's impatience. "I'll see that you get your hankie back," she said as she stuffed it in her bag, then stepped into the main hall to leave. Clay's voice stopped her.

"You got a place to stay?"

Willa looked up at Clay, surprised. "The motel I stayed at last night may still have a vacancy."

"Good." He nodded, clearly satisfied with her answer. Willa suddenly understood.

"Don't worry, Clay. I wouldn't think of imposing on my cousin."

"Just so you don't get it in your head to take advantage of either her or Tess," he said, his hard gaze pinning hers. "They're both too vulnerable right now."

Willa felt a spurt of anger. "So you're their self-appointed protector," she concluded mockingly, her lips twisting. "If I were you, I'd mind my own business."

Clay's eyes glittered. "You are my business," he growled. "And until you leave town permanently, I plan to keep an eye on you."

"I'm sure Paige will have something to say about that," Willa retorted, having already guessed Paige and Clay were either involved or about to be. The thought galled her.

"You're the last woman Paige needs to be jealous of."

Willa gave him a wry smile. "Paige won't be jealous, Clay. She'll be worried."

Willa's implication lay heavily in the sudden silence between them. Clay's dark gaze was livid with rage and a muscle worked wildly in his jaw as he glared down at her.

"You aren't a seventeen-year-old kid this time, Willa," he said in a low, burning voice. "This time you'll pay for anything you do. I'll see to it."

Willa's eyes were overbright as the bitterness and sense of betrayal that had festered inside her for five years surged to the surface. "Just make sure you've got all the facts," she said, then added pointedly, "this time."

Willa turned and walked briskly down the hall to the elevators, her heart little more than a throbbing wound in her chest.

The pain hadn't subsided by the time she'd ordered a take-out sandwich at the café down the street from the hospital, then made her way back to the small road-side motel at the edge of town.

Bleakly she stared at the cold, deli-style sandwich, unable to eat more than a couple of bites. The hot coffee tasted good, its warmth taking the edge off her raw feelings, but nothing could quite deaden the twisting sense of betrayal that churned within her.

It was a good thing, she realized now, that she'd repressed much of the devastation she'd experienced after Angie's death when Clay had turned against her. She wouldn't have been able to bear up half so well these past years if she hadn't. It had been bad enough that Uncle Cal had automatically sided with Paige, unable to believe that his precious daughter was anything less than perfect; when most of the friends Willa thought she and her cousin shared had taken Paige's side, she'd been crushed.

But when Clay joined the rest, choosing to believe Paige instead of her, that had been the final blow. Surely he'd known her better than that, she thought despairingly.

Clay's defection had been a betrayal of her trust and deep affection for him. In the more than seven years she and Angie had been best friends—and almost inseparable—she'd never once lied to Clay. Oh, she and Angie had both been a handful, their good-humored pranks often directed toward him, but he'd treated her like a second little sister. Willa had idolized him.

When Angie was killed and Willa was blamed for her death, she'd lost everyone she loved, including Clay. The compounded grief had been almost more than she could bear.

Willa rose suddenly from her chair, wadding the sandwich into its wrapper before flinging it into the trash.

"What does it matter, anyway?" she demanded of herself aloud as she savagely raked her trembling fingers through her hair. Though she hadn't caused Angie's death, she hadn't been able to save her life, either. The horror of that truth would haunt her for the rest of her life.

"YOU'RE LOOKING MUCH BETTER today, Aunt Tess," Willa offered quietly, all too aware of Paige's sullen presence at the other side of the bed.

A week had gone by since the funeral, a week since her aunt had first been admitted to the hospital. Today was her second day out of the Cardiac Care Unit and in her own private room. The doctor had assured them all that in spite of the fact that Tess's recovery would be slower than normal due to her grief over her husband's death, she was doing well, and Willa's relief knew no bounds.

On the other hand, now that Tess was recovering, Willa would have to think about leaving soon. And judging by the killing looks Paige flashed her every now and then, soon was not nearly quick enough.

"I'm feeling much, much better, Willa," Tess said, her eyes twinkling fondly as she gazed at her niece. "Having you back has been like a tonic."

Willa shoved her hands into her jeans pockets, suddenly nervous. Every time she had been allowed into the CCU to visit her aunt, Tess had talked as if Willa were back in Cascade for good. Willa's gentle hints to the contrary were always met by such confusion and distress that she feared she might be adversely affecting her aunt's health. Was now a good time to reintroduce the idea that she would soon have to head back to Colorado?

"I've got a woman coming in today to do your hair for you, Mother," Paige interjected before either of them could speak again. "Think how good it will feel to have it washed and done up."

"You already mentioned it, Paige," Tess said, her eyes never leaving Willa's. "Right now, I want to talk to Willa about the ranch before I run out of steam."

Paige's face paled. "Please, Mother, don't."

Tess glanced over at her daughter and Willa witnessed a stubbornness she'd not known her aunt to be capable of. Willa was intrigued.

"We went over this last night, Paige, and I don't want to rehash any of it. In another week, you'll be going on a new assignment for that modeling agency and I'll be stuck here without anyone to keep an eye on things. From what Willa's told me about the place she's working, she'd be perfect for the job." Tess turned her head and looked at Willa, catching the surprise on Willa's face as the true meaning of the words dawned on her.

While Tess had asked a number of questions about Willa's life and what she was doing now, her questions had been more specifically about Willa's abilities. The way people in Cascade seemed to feel about her, Willa hadn't been comfortable confiding all the details of her life to anyone, not even her aunt. And now, with Paige hovering in the room, Willa was not about to mention that she was half-owner of the D & R Ranch.

"I need your help, Willa," Tess began earnestly, her eyes searching hers. "Ever since Cal took sick four years back, the ranch hasn't been doing very well. We had to let go of all but two of the hands. One quit a few weeks ago. The other—" Tess shook her head "—has a problem with liquor. He says he only does his drinking in the bunkhouse or in town, but he's come in for a meal plenty of times smelling of whiskey. Of course, even if he was sober I don't think he could handle things," Tess added.

Willa somehow had to forestall the question she sensed Tess was leading up to. She opened her mouth to decline, but the pained entreaty in her aunt's eyes stopped her.

"I need someone to take over for me or I'll lose everything. Cal worked so hard for that ranch. I can't lose it now." Her soft gray eyes grew misty. "I know you've got hard feelings against Cal, but it would mean an awful lot to me if you'd stay on and help out."

"Mother," Paige murmured crossly, "we don't need her."

"I need her," Tess said firmly, the mistiness fading as she overruled her daughter.

Willa couldn't believe what she was hearing. Never mind the fact that her aunt had grown a bit more assertive over the years; she was not only asking Willa to stay, but to take on a job even an experienced rancher would find a challenge. It was hard enough these days to turn a profit in ranching, but to be asked to stabilize a ranch that was in trouble was an undertaking that Willa wasn't sure she was any match for.

The D & R was about the same size operation as the Harding ranch and she'd managed that, but if the Circle H was too far gone, she wasn't certain good management was enough to bring it back. She and Ivy had started out breaking even and had been careful to avoid most of the pitfalls that might have put them under a crippling debt load. Staying profitable was much, much easier than forcing a losing operation to pay. Besides, she and Ivy had always worked as a team. This time she'd be on her own. Her first instinct was to decline her aunt's request.

"I don't think I'm the person for the job, Auntie," Willa said, wanting to let her aunt down gently.

"I can't think of anyone better," Tess countered. "And you'd be home, Willa. That's something I've wanted since the day Cal sent you away."

"I'm not sure I could handle it," Willa admitted. "If the Circle H is in too much trouble, I might not be able to help you hang on to it, anyway. You need someone with a lot more experience than I have." Even if she took the job there was no guarantee that she would be able to save the failing ranch. If it failed, anyway, after she took over, she knew she'd automatically be blamed. Willa didn't want to be assigned that kind of responsibility.

"Paige has offered to put some of her money into it, at least to take care of wages and repairs. That should help a lot. But she—"

"I offered to put a sizable amount of money into the ranch if you could find a competent foreman," Paige corrected. "I'm not at all convinced that Willa's competent. What does a female hired hand know about managing a ranch? Besides, you said she works with horses. Ours is a cattle operation. It's a job for a man."

"You know better than that, Paige," Tess chided, shaking her head. "You know I'm not much on this women's lib stuff, but I don't see any sense in a woman holding back from a man's job if it's what she wants and she can do it. Besides, Willa was working alongside your father and his hired men when you were still playing with dolls. If there's something she doesn't know about ranching, it's not much."

Tess's outspoken confidence brought a lump to Willa's throat.

"All right then, Mother," Paige said, tossing her dark mane of hair defiantly, "I'll make it clearer. I don't want Willa here."

The fatigue that had gradually crept over Aunt Tess's face was suddenly dispelled, and her soft eyes went stern. "Your father was wrong to send Willa away, Paige. There wasn't a day went by that I didn't regret letting him have his way. Now that she's back—" Tess turned to Willa, her gaze growing warm as she put out her hand and grasped Willa's "—I'm determined to find some way to keep her here."

Willa's lips moved into a tremulous smile as she squeezed her aunt's hand.

"Please, Willa," Tess coaxed. "At least go out to the ranch and look things over."

Willa's eyes shied from the hopeful look on her aunt's face. "Even if I said yes, what about Clay Cantrell?"

"Yes, Mother," Paige stepped in eagerly. "What about Clay? How do you think he'd feel with Willa around—as a reminder?"

Willa stiffened and flashed a look across the bed, unable to keep from glaring at her cousin. Her cheeks took on a dull flush as she saw the smug look on Paige's expertly made-up face. Suddenly, more than anything, Willa wanted to make that smug look disappear.

"All right, Auntie," she heard herself say. Her eyes came back to catch the excited look in her aunt's. "I'll go out and take a look at the Circle H. But before I decide, I want to talk to Clay."

The lines of age and stress on her aunt's face relaxed. "I'll give him a call."

"No, Aunt Tess," Willa said firmly. "If I decide to stay, Clay and I will have to get along without a go-between. I'll talk to him."

"All right, Willa. Handle it your way. I trust you."

Willa suddenly felt uncomfortable with her aunt's overstated confidence in her, wary of what she expected. "I want you to understand that this arrangement won't be permanent." Willa's heart sank as she saw that her caution had no dampening effect on her aunt's enthusiasm. It was as if Tess were ignoring any words she didn't want to hear. Willa had to make it clearer.

"I'll only fill in until things get straightened out and I can find a good foreman for you."

Aunt Tess's brow wrinkled only slightly at Willa's words. "We'll work something out," she said as she leaned back against her pillows, her strength waning.

Neither saw the look of fear that crossed Paige's lovely features.

CLAY CANTRELL'S Orion Ranch lay just to the south of the much smaller Circle H. Willa could have taken a horse and ridden to the house in a bit more than half the time it would take her to drive her car from the Circle H ranch house to the highway, then over to the Orion Ranch, but the days when little formality was observed had died with Angie.

Willa knew she wouldn't be welcome at Orion, though just how unwelcome remained to be seen. At the moment, she was too furious to care.

She was worn out and discouraged, angry over the condition of the Circle H. She'd driven out to the ranch as her aunt had asked, and was truly shocked by the run-down appearance of the house and buildings. Everything could stand a fresh coat of paint and easily half the corrals near the barn were becoming overgrown with weeds. Old wind damage done to the barn roof had not been repaired and the resulting leak had produced several moldy bales of hay in the loft.

Signs of waste and laziness were everywhere, from the sloppy storage of hay and feed to the poorly kept stalls in the barn that hadn't been mucked out properly for weeks. The stench had been overpowering.

Then she'd met Art Boles, the Circle H's hired hand, and had been outraged at both his drunken state and his bad manners. He'd refused to cooperate with her, the insolence in his gaze challenging her right to any information. The few answers he'd supplied to her many questions had been evasive at best. Willa had finally selected and saddled a horse, then ridden out alone to look over as much of the ranch as possible that afternoon.

There wasn't a fence on the place that didn't need some kind of repair. Cattle that should have been accustomed to being worked were as wild as deer and almost as elusive. Willa's outrage mounted when she caught sight of at least three unbranded calves that, judging from their sizes, had been born well before spring roundup and therefore, should already have been carrying the Circle H brand.

When she'd at last returned to the barn and asked Art Boles to see to her horse, he'd grudgingly done so, while she headed for the machine shed to look over the equipment. At least everything there had seemed in good shape. Until she'd got to the tractor and discovered parts of its engine had been disassembled—ostensibly to make a repair—then been left lying on a bench nearby.

In a matter of days, the hay pasture would need to be cut and baled, but the tractor was out of commission and apparently had been for quite some time. If this was more of Art Boles's handiwork, there was no telling whether the tractor would ever be serviceable again.

Willa had stomped over to the bunkhouse in a fine fury. This time Boles was defensive, his manner bordering on belligerence.

"Too much work for one man," he'd grumbled. "And what the hell gives you the right to come snoopin' around here, anyway? Who did you say you was?"

Willa hadn't been taken in by his sudden bout of amnesia. "We discussed who I was and why I was here hours ago, Mr. Boles. What we haven't discussed is what you've been doing to earn your wages."

Art Boles had drawn himself up and blustered, "I don't have to answer to you."

Willa had nodded in agreement, her mouth set in a sour slash. "That may change, Mr. Boles. If it does, I can assure you that you won't have to answer to me long, since you'll be out of a job." Not trusting herself to keep from ordering him off the Circle H at that very moment, Willa had turned and gone to her car. It sickened her to think that Art Boles had been collecting the wages Tess had been hard put to pay, while he'd given very little work in exchange.

Willa was reminded of Clay's eagerness to make sure she didn't take advantage of her aunt. He'd threatened to keep a close eye on her, when all the time he'd overlooked what Art Boles had been doing. Willa made up her mind to point that out to him if he objected too strongly to her staying on at the Circle H.

Because she was going to stay, she'd decided. Tess did need her help, if for nothing more than to fire Art Boles and hire her a competent foreman and one or two conscientious ranch hands. Surely Clay could bear to put up with her presence in his part of the country for a few weeks. She had little doubt that Ivy could manage the D & R without her for a while, since their foreman, Deke Bailey, could easily fill in for Willa.

Too soon she reached the turnoff and in less time than she remembered, she was braking to a stop in front of the Cantrell ranch house.

Designed to harmonize with the natural terrain, the house was built from trees grown on the ranch itself, the long, thick logs giving the sprawling single-story structure a formidable ruggedness and a feeling of permanence.

Willa had spent a lot of time in that house and on this ranch. She and Angie had been fast friends, the fact that they were the same age and had both been orphaned linking them together in a very special way. Bright, enthusiastic, irrepressible, they'd both been a challenge for Clay, who seemed to be the only one who could tolerate their antics for long. Willa had envied Angie her elder brother until she'd matured enough to develop a mild crush on him.

From then on, Clay had become a romantic curiosity, fueling her adolescent daydreams and presenting Willa with what she considered a safe challenge for her rapidly developing feminine charms. The day she decided to unleash those charms on him was the day she learned that it wasn't safe to play kissing games with Clay Cantrell.

Willa's lips curved slightly. She was unable even in the face of a bitter encounter with Clay to suppress the recollection. He'd had too great an influence on her growing up, had claimed too much of her affection for Willa to totally banish his memory. No matter what the outcome of this visit, Clay, like Angie, would always claim a lion's share of her love.

Willa's anger faded. She didn't want her presence to hurt Clay. Perhaps there was a way to convince him to tolerate her long enough for her to help her aunt get the ranch back on the rails. Clay had always been a reasonable man and it was certain he had a sizable soft spot for her aunt and cousin, even if he could no longer summon any fondness for her. Maybe that would be enough.

Leaving the keys in the ignition, Willa opened her car door and stepped out, hoping the warm, early evening breeze had carried the sound of her arrival into the house. She'd known better than to phone Clay to ask his permission to come here, but she didn't want to take him too much by surprise.

She went up the front walk to the door, hesitating only a moment more before she knocked. She waited a bit, chafed a nervous palm against her jeans, then knocked again. The door opened just as she lowered her hand.

"Hello, Clay."

Clay Cantrell's six-foot-four height filled the doorway, the breadth of his shoulders taking up a good share of its width. He didn't seem surprised to see her, but his eyes held a cold challenge.

"I'd like to talk to you, if I may," she said, resolving to cling to her good memories of him rather than dwell on the animosity he held toward her now. Clay had been a good friend once, and though he'd betrayed her friendship by believing the worst about her, even she had to admit that the grim circumstances back then would have pushed any friendship to the breaking point. "Please, Clay," she added softly.

The moments ticked by, until Willa was certain he wasn't going to allow her into his house. At last he stood aside and gestured for her to enter.

The moment Willa crossed the threshold it was like stepping backward in time. Nothing had changed inside the large, ruggedly furnished room, from the heavy leather and wood furniture to the American Indian artifacts that decorated the walls and the heavy woven rugs scattered here and there on the polished wood floor. Willa's eyes went instantly to the mantel above the stone fireplace.

Angie's high school graduation picture was still there. Though Angie had been killed only a few weeks before graduation, she and Willa had had their portraits done months earlier.

The ache of grief and regret that had never totally left Willa came pulsing back as she was reminded that the other portrait that had once shared pride of place on that mantel—her own—had been removed.

"You said you wanted to talk."

Clay's deep voice startled her and she turned quickly toward the somber-faced man. There was no hint of softness in his flinty expression, just an impenetrable hardness that reminded her of the last time she'd stood before him in this room—the time she'd tried to tell him about the accident. He'd been drinking heavily that night. "Get out of this house!" he'd roared, too grief stricken at the sight of her to allow her even a moment to explain before he grabbed her arm and ushered her roughly to the door. She had been inconsolable.

Suddenly the longing to again try telling Clay what had really happened when Angie was killed—and to at last be believed—was overwhelming. Was the lie he'd accepted five years earlier still stronger than the truth? Did she have the courage to find out?

The memory of her aunt collapsing in the cemetery brought Willa back to reality. What would it do to Tess if she were to again insist that Paige's reckless driving had caused the accident? Tess's love for her daughter and pride in her were enormous. The mere suggestion of the truth could be enough to seriously threaten her aunt's life.

Willa felt the old helplessness stir. She could say nothing. In the eyes of everyone in and around Cascade, and particularly in Clay's, she would have to remain the spineless little liar who'd repaid her aunt and uncle for taking her in by telling horrible lies about their darling Paige. Besides, Clay had already made his choice. Five years earlier, Willa had been prepared to beg him to believe her. But she wouldn't beg him now—or ever. Pride stiffened her spine. She would never again plead for anyone's trust.

"I suppose Paige called to tell you why I'm here," she began, already sensing Paige had.

"She called earlier today. Said Tess had asked you to stay on and take over the Circle H." Clay's voice was bitterly cynical.

"Then you also know that Tess asked me to go out and look things over, and that I might be stopping by," she said.

"She told me that, too."

"I've decided to stay," Willa said simply, shoving her nervous fingers into her jeans pockets.

"No."

Willa felt her heart recoil at that one word, spoken so softly, yet so harshly.

"The Circle H is in bad shape," Willa persisted. "I plan to stay just long enough to help straighten things out for Aunt Tess and find someone reliable to take over. I doubt if I'd be around for more than a month at the outside."

Clay gave a sarcastic chuckle. "What could you do?"

Willa's chin lifted at his skepticism as she declared softly, "A lot more than my aunt's many friends and neighbors have done."

Clay's hard expression didn't alter; he must have expected her to say something like that. "Tess's too damned proud to allow much help."

"She's always been that way," Willa agreed. "But she's asked for my help. I want to do it, Clay. I'd like to try."

Clay couldn't help but read the shadowy longing in Willa's green eyes. Her face was stiff and her lips were pressed together with the effort she made to hide her feelings from him. He knew that look as well as he'd known her once upon a time. Those big green eyes had always managed to betray enough of what was going on in her pretty head that he'd teased her frequently about being able to read her like a book. Their relationship had evolved into a game of sorts, one that they'd both played at, a shallow flirtation that had permitted him to harmlessly assuage his attraction to her.

Clay felt himself grow cold. He didn't want to remember that or anything else about Willa Ross. He wanted to harden himself to everything about her but the more he tried the more difficult it became. The seventeen-year-old imp he'd been half in love with was gone; in her place was this serious, melancholy young woman who looked as if she never smiled or had a carefree thought. It was because he could tell that she was trying to conceal it all from him and not play on his sympathy that he felt something penetrate his bitterness and sink deeply into his heart.

"Then I reckon we'd both better stay out of each other's way," he growled irritably as he turned away and pushed a calloused hand through his dark hair.

The painful tension in her body eased with relief, but Willa suddenly felt unbearably sad.

I don't want to hurt you, Clay, she wanted to say. *If there were any way I could go back to that day and do just one tiny thing different . . .*

Willa was glad he couldn't see her face just then. "Tess will be relieved. Thanks." Willa stared a moment more at that proud set of shoulders before she turned and left quietly.

CHAPTER THREE

WILLA WAS UP EARLY the next morning. She'd been unable to reach her partner, Ivy Dayton, by phone the night before, so she made the call as soon as she got up, hoping to catch Ivy before she left the house.

"Take whatever time you need," Ivy said without hesitation after Willa had related the details of her aunt's situation. "Deke and I can hire some summer help if we need to."

"Thanks a lot, Ivy. I really appreciate it."

"Shucks, it's no more'n you'd do for me," Ivy said dismissively, and Willa smiled at the image she had of her red-haired, freckle-faced friend, who was almost eight years her senior. Ivy was a big-hearted country girl, generous to a fault, just a bit flamboyant, but savvy and as tough as nails when it came to doing business. "You just take care of yourself up there."

"Don't worry. I've grown up some in the past five years," Willa replied, not needing to say more since Ivy knew everything.

Ivy gave an inelegant snort. "So has that cousin of yours. Now that you're back she's bound to be nervous as a weasel and twice as sneaky. You already know what she's capable of when it comes to saving her own hide."

Willa grimaced at the reminder but was grateful for Ivy's unswerving loyalty. She and Ivy had worked together for a year on a big ranch in Kansas before Ivy had suggested a partnership that would pool their talents and their money. Though widowed at twenty-five, Ivy had managed to save most of the money from her husband's estate, and with what she'd put away of her earnings, had been ready to buy something of her own. By then, Willa had already confided her past to Ivy, and it was Ivy's steadfast friendship and belief in her that had eased the pain of estrangement from family and friends that Willa had felt so acutely.

"I'll be careful, Ivy. Thanks."

"Let me know if you need anything."

"I will. Call you in another week or so," Willa said, then returned the phone to its cradle.

It didn't take long to pack and check out of the motel. Though it was still too early to visit her aunt, Willa managed to slip into her room just as Dr. Elliot finished Tess's morning exam and was about to leave.

"Visiting hours don't start for another couple of hours, young lady," he scolded, though the smile on his face negated his gruff tone. Dr. Elliot's attitude toward her had softened considerably in the past few days, and Willa smiled back easily.

"Five minutes?"

"Let's just don't make it a habit," he said, then exited briskly from the room.

"You've decided to say," Tess concluded, a sunny smile on her face. Tess looked even better this morning and Willa marveled at her growing improvement.

"I have. But only for a few weeks—a month, maybe," Willa cautioned gently. "I can only take so much time from my job."

Tess's brow furrowed slightly. "You enjoy working with horses then. Well, there's no reason the Circle H can't begin to make a changeover to horse breeding,'' she reasoned and Willa went tense.

Panicked by her aunt's seeming determination for her to stay permanently, yet realizing that Tess might not be ready to face the shock of learning that her niece's prior obligations went much farther than those of a hired hand, Willa spoke quickly. "Let's just wait and see, Aunt Tess. Any decisions like that should be made later when you're better and we see how things go."

Willa didn't add that there were no guarantees the Circle H could survive. And since she hadn't yet gone over the books or delved too deeply into just how dire the ranch's finances were, she didn't want to paint too discouraging a picture, either. If she could, she intended to shelter her aunt from as much worry and unpleasantness as possible.

"Did you talk to Clay?"

"I went over to Orion last night. There won't be any problem with him." Willa was confident of that. Clay might object to her staying on, and there would naturally be some unpleasant moments between the two of them, but he wouldn't deliberately cause trouble.

"Good." Tess leaned back against her pillows. "I want you to stop by the lawyer's office today and see what needs to be done for you to get into the ranch accounts and handle my business. He should have everything ready for you to sign. When are you going to move into the house?"

"Later today. I've got a few errands to do in town after I talk to your lawyer."

Tess nodded her approval. "Paige has been staying with some of her friends, so you might need to buy groceries. And Willa—" Tess looked troubled

"—whatever you decide to do about Art Boles is fine with me."

"Don't worry, Aunt Tess. I can handle him." Willa forced her lips into a curve to allay her aunt's concern. Actually, firing Art Boles was a task she didn't look forward to, but neither did she want to have a man like him working on the Circle H.

"If you get too busy, don't worry about driving all the way back to town tonight for visiting hours. You'll likely be tired," Tess predicted.

"I'll give you a call if I can't make it," Willa said, and after a few last words, she left the hospital.

"I JUST HOPE YOU KNOW what you're doing firing Art Boles," Paige said snidely from the doorway, cigarette in hand. Willa glanced up from the books she'd been poring over all evening, frowning at the reminder of the scene Art Boles had made that afternoon after she'd fired him and handed him a check for the balance of his wages. "He was probably the only cowhand in the county who'd work for you."

"He wasn't working, period," Willa reminded her cousin. "What do you want, Paige?" she demanded ungraciously, not feeling particularly obliged to be polite. She was tired and planned to be up at first light the next morning.

"I'd like to talk," Paige answered, sauntering into the room and picking up the small crystal ashtray that sat on the corner of the desk at which Willa was working.

"I'm not too interested in anything you have to say," Willa said coldly as she closed the ledgers and stacked them. She wasn't thrilled that Paige had decided to return to the ranch earlier that day.

"You might be, Cousin," Paige went on haughtily, having perched her long, elegant body on the arm of the nearest wing chair. Chicly clad in a blue silk dress that Willa was certain was a designer original, Paige looked every bit the fashion model. The stunning combination of long, wavy raven tresses, clear luminescent skin and exotic violet eyes made her a natural. Willa had no idea how well Paige had done for herself, since she hadn't been in contact with her aunt these past years, but there was a sophisticated, well-cared-for look about Paige that fairly shouted success. "If you and I can't come to some kind of understanding, Mother's going to be the one who suffers the most."

"Scared?" Willa challenged, though the realization brought her little satisfaction. In spite of what Paige had done, Willa hated the antagonism between them. She knew instinctively that she suffered the ill will they bore each other much more acutely than Paige.

Paige's face flushed with guilt and resentment, but she didn't respond to Willa's taunt. "I'm sure you realize how precarious mother's health is."

Willa came to her feet and grabbed up the ledgers. "How convenient for you," she murmured as she turned away and shoved them into the low cabinet beneath the double windows.

"It could literally kill Mother if you were to start trouble," Paige persisted.

Willa struggled to suppress her anger as she turned to face her cousin. "I get the message."

"That's good," Paige said, her brow arched. Then, to Willa's surprise, Paige's haughty look altered. "For what it's worth, Willa, I'm sorry."

Willa couldn't have been more shocked, but managed to keep it to herself.

"I was terrified of what would happen to me if I told the truth," Paige began, then shrugged uncomfortably. "You were always so strong and so brave, I thought you'd survive it all better than I could. And since Clay was your friend, I was certain he'd forgive you a lot more easily than he'd forgive me." Paige was watching Willa closely. "I had no idea Daddy would throw you out or that people would react as strongly as they all did." Paige hesitated before her chin went up defensively. "If it makes any difference, I would have come forward if Clay had decided to press charges."

Willa stared, unable to fully believe what she was hearing. She knew instinctively that she was the only one who had ever heard this confession and strongly suspected Paige would not only never repeat it, but would hereafter insist even more vigorously that Willa had been at fault.

"I don't think you would have admitted the truth even then, Paige," Willa scoffed. "If you couldn't tell your own mother and father the truth, I doubt you would have had the courage to face going to court and risk being placed in some kind of juvenile detention until you were eighteen."

"My life would have been ruined," Paige snapped, dropping all pretense of contrition. "You didn't have any big ambitions. All you ever wanted to do was live on a ranch someplace like a common cowhand."

"So my future didn't count," Willa concluded grimly, then shook her head. "Cal and Tess worshipped you, Paige. They loved you as much as any parents could love their child. I don't think there was anything they would have denied you. How is it you turned out so wrong?''

Paige's face reddened as she bent her head and crushed her cigarette out violently in the ashtray.

"Just remember what I said about Mother," she warned as her head came up and she pinned Willa with an icy stare. "And don't plan to stay around too long."

Paige rose from the chair arm, tossed down the ashtray, then swept regally from the room.

WILLA SPENT the next two days mucking out the barn and readying the loft for hay before she patched the barn roof. She'd hired a mechanic to come to the ranch and repair the tractor, then had him take a look at her uncle's old red pickup while he was there. Getting the pickup in good driving order had cost more than Willa had anticipated, but the truck was a necessity, and the price of a new one was well beyond what her aunt could afford this year. Willa cringed as she calculated that it wouldn't be too many more months before the truck would need new tires.

So far, there had been little response to the ads she'd placed locally for a foreman and ranch hands. She'd had a couple of calls from Casper and Cheyenne, but it would be next week before any of the respondents from outside Cascade could get to the Circle H for an interview. In the meantime, she had estimated the cost of repairs around the ranch and had decided to get started buying supplies.

Willa became so absorbed in her solitary ranch work that she managed to set aside any uneasy thoughts she'd had about doing business in the small community. Though she visited her aunt daily, she'd had little contact with anyone beyond Paige and the hospital staff. Consequently, her first trip to the lumberyard to buy barbed wire and fence posts was an abrupt awakening.

"I believe I was next," she said firmly as she stepped up to the counter and the short man in blue coveralls, who was in charge of writing up the orders. In spite of the fact that she'd been one of the first to arrive that morning, the man had ignored her to wait on other customers. Taken aback by the clerk's deliberate rudeness, she'd not been quite able to believe she was actually being snubbed, until his repeated oversights became too blatant to be ignored.

"You'll have to wait your turn, miss," he said, then looked past her to the next person in line.

"I have waited my turn," Willa insisted, raising her voice just enough to be heard by everyone in the vicinity as she stepped aside to block the man behind her from moving forward. The quiet conversations around them ceased, and when the clerk flushed self-consciously, Willa sensed everyone's attention was on them.

"I need fifteen rolls of wire and about one hundred wood posts," she said briskly, staring challengingly at the clerk until his gaze veered from hers to glance over her left shoulder.

Intuition sent a sharp tingle through her and she turned her head, her lips tightening as she caught sight of Clay Cantrell standing a few feet away. Concluding that he'd been among those who had entered the store after her and that he had probably seen everything that had gone on, she returned her attention to the clerk.

"Obviously your company can afford to lose business from the Circle H," she said, then turned away, incensed that taking her business to the lumberyard in the next town meant driving her uncle's pickup and trailer almost ninety extra miles.

She'd walked halfway to the door, when the clerk called out to her. "Miss Ross? Did you say fifteen rolls of wire and one hundred wood fence posts?" Willa halted, turned, then noted that Clay was now nowhere in sight. To her surprise, the clerk was bustling toward her, hastily scrawling her order on his clipboard. "If you'll just pay for this up front, you can pick up your order in the yard." The man hurriedly initialed the papers and held them toward her expectantly, his low "Sorry for the delay, miss" apologetic enough to induce her to take them.

Without so much as a glance at anyone, Willa collected the rest of the hardware items on her list, paid for them, then went out to drive the truck and small trailer into the yard behind the store to be loaded. Fortunately her trip to the feed store went better, as did her trip to pick up a few groceries, which she placed in the cab next to the small cooler she'd brought along to stow perishables in. By the time she'd gone to the bank and opened a personal checking account it was well past lunchtime, and Willa stopped at a small restaurant on the outskirts of Cascade.

A favorite of hers when she was growing up, Cristy's had been the best place in town for hamburgers and tenderloins, and Willa looked forward to reacquainting herself with one of the hot sandwiches Cristy's was known for.

The moment she walked into the restaurant she saw Clay sitting with three other men at a table toward the front, the remnants of his lunch before him as he lingered over a cup of coffee. He hadn't seen her yet, so she glanced around, looking for a place to sit. Though the lunch counter was filled and the dining area crowded, Willa managed to find a small empty booth midway back. The waitress, whom Willa recognized from years before as Laureen, bustled up, set down a glass of water and started to hand Willa a menu, when she suddenly stopped.

Willa had reached up for the menu and taken hold of it before Laureen's tight expression registered. A testing tug of the menu told Willa the woman was having second thoughts about giving it to her. Only after an awkward moment did the waitress release the menu and murmur a perfunctory greeting before turning and rushing away.

Willa scarcely looked at the menu once she saw that her favorite dishes were still listed. She laid the menu down to indicate her readiness to order, but sat there for more than ten minutes before Laureen started in her direction. Then, coffeepot in hand, the waitress worked the tables and booths in her area, adroitly managing to ignore Willa in much the same way she'd been ignored at the lumberyard.

Embarrassment and anger brought a high flush to Willa's cheeks as she glanced around and noticed the number of curious eyes fixed on her that suddenly looked down or away. The only pair of eyes that didn't shy from hers were the expressionless black ones that watched her from the table near the front of the restaurant.

Willa realized that Clay had seen her shortly after she'd come in and that he'd been watching her for quite some time when his gaze traveled from her to

Laureen as the woman continued to avoid taking her order.

Just then Laureen glanced in Clay's direction as if seeking approval. That brief meeting of gazes was all Willa needed to see. With stiff dignity, she slid to the edge of the booth, then rose to walk calmly to the door. Inwardly she was seething with a chaotic mixture of hurt and barely controlled anger, but she was careful not to let it show on her face.

She'd not thought Clay capable of using his influence to cause her problems and public embarrassment, but he clearly had that day, at least twice. Or had he? Perhaps she would have been treated the same whether he'd been present or not. Perhaps this was the way of some to indicate their allegiance to Clay and their sympathy for the pain her presence might be causing him.

Cascade was a small rural town, and as such was subject to the same kind of attitudes and prejudices common to most small towns. Willa guessed that many people in the area believed she'd got off too easily when Angie was killed, and now felt quite justified in dealing out a bit of vengeance on Angie's behalf. It saddened Willa to recall that she'd known most of these people once. Cascade was a good, close-knit community, made up of good, law-abiding people. Knowing that made the injustice of their actions doubly hard to take. Willa had to admit now that Paige's fear of being socially ostracized was well-founded, though it in no way excused the actions she'd taken to avoid it.

Willa walked to the truck and made a quick check that the load was secure inside the trailer before she got behind the wheel and started for the ranch.

Either way, there wasn't much she could do about what people thought of her except get on with her job. The sooner the ranch was doing better and she found someone capable to run it, the sooner she could leave and go back to Colorado, where she was welcome and her word was worth something.

She was almost a mile from the turnoff to the Orion Ranch, when she glanced into her side mirror and saw a big silver-and-black pickup gaining steadily on her much slower truck and trailer.

Just at the moment she was distracted her truck seemed to hit a hard bump. Startled, Willa jerked her attention back to the road as the truck lapsed into the staccato jarring that indicated a flat tire. Moaning in disgust, Willa slowed the vehicle, then pulled carefully onto the graveled shoulder. The silver-and-black pickup whizzed on past as she brought her truck to a stop but left the engine running.

Willa grabbed her work gloves from the seat, resigned to unhitching the trailer and unloading the heavy spools of wire from the truck bed before she could begin to change the tire. When she got out, she noted unhappily that the left rear tire rim was already resting on the deflated remains of the rubber.

She reached into the back of the truck bed for a cement block to place beneath the wagon tongue of the trailer to keep it elevated while she unhitched it and disconnected the trailer lights. As a precaution, she slid a fence post behind the trailer tires to keep the trailer from rolling away on the slight incline. Once she got back into the truck and moved it forward a few feet, she switched off the engine, set the brake, then got out to place a block just ahead of one of the front tires of the pickup to keep it steady while she changed

the tire. She had just let down the tailgate of the truck
to unload the wire, when she heard a vehicle approach.

The silver-and-black pickup that had passed her
moments earlier was coming back down the highway
toward her. Since she didn't expect it to stop, she
climbed onto the tailgate and reached for the first
spool of wire. To her surprise, the vehicle slowed, then
turned onto the graveled shoulder, where it stopped
headlight to headlight with her truck. Willa was startled when she saw who was driving.

Clay Cantrell opened the door, then stepped down,
and Willa guessed from the fixed line of his mouth
that he had felt obligated to come back and lend his
assistance, no matter how distasteful he found the
idea. The dark sunglasses he wore probably hid a
wealth of loathing for her. She could well imagine the
cold unfriendly depths of those midnight-black eyes,
and decided that very instant to refuse any offer of
help.

Just as she bent down to maneuver the spool of wire
to the edge of the tailgate so she could lower it to the
ground, Clay reached into the truck and took hold of
it.

"I can get it," she said quickly, her green eyes
flashing in his direction as she held the spool immov-
able. Clay ignored her and gave the spool a yank that
dared her to get into a tug-of-war with him. "I don't
need your help."

The stern line of Clay's mouth slanted humor-
lessly, but he made no response. Instead he moved the
spool to the tailgate then lowered it to the ground.

"I mean it, Clay," she said as he leaned back into the truck to reach for the next spool. "I don't need your help."

"You get it, anyway," he snarled as he reached in and got a grip on one of the spools. "Are you going to get busy, or do I have to do this alone?" Before she could respond, he was pulling the roll past her forcing Willa to step aside to assist him. In no time, they had unloaded all the rolls.

"Thanks," she said grudgingly. "I can take care of the rest myself."

Giving every impression that he hadn't heard a word, Clay slammed the tailgate shut, then got down on one knee to get the spare tire from the rack beneath the truck bed. "You gotta jack?" he growled as he worked.

"Yes, but I can take care of things now," Willa repeated as she started to kneel down to reach for the spare herself.

Clay's icy voice stopped her. "I haven't got the time or the patience to argue with you, Willa."

Willa hesitated, then straightened and stalked off to get the jack and lug wrench from behind the seat in the cab, intending to refuse any further help. When she returned with the tools, Clay dropped the spare on the ground, letting it wobble and fall onto its side.

"This one's damn near as flat as the other one," he said, depressing the wall of the tire with the toe of his boot. Willa watched, a sinking sensation in her stomach as the new problem registered.

Willa tossed the tools down, then raised her arm to blot the perspiration from her forehead with her sleeve. What a predicament she was in. She wasn't so foolish as to refuse Clay's help now, not when her only other choice was to walk the five or six miles back to town in the heat and take the chance that someone would make off with the fencing while she was getting the spare fixed. It stung to realize she wasn't quite as self-sufficient as she'd thought, but what really stung was the fact that she was in a position that made it more sensible to ask Clay for his help than to spurn it. Assuming, that is, he was still of a mind to give it. Choking back a good bit of her pride, she dropped her arm and looked up at him, seeing twin images of herself reflected in his dark glasses.

"You don't happen to have a portable air tank in the back of your truck, do you?" she asked, forced to set aside any lingering resistance to his help.

"Probably wouldn't do any good," he said, reaching down to grip the spindle hole and lift the useless spare before he carried it to the trailer and laid it on top of the fence posts. That done, he turned and walked to his truck without another word.

Shocked that he was apparently leaving her to her own devices along the deserted stretch of highway, Willa could only stare for a moment. Then, determined not to let him just drive away, she hurried after him.

"I can pay you to haul the wire and the trailer to the Circle H, Clay," she said as she caught up with him.

"I don't want your money," he grumbled as he walked around to the back of his pickup.

"I can't just leave that fencing here," she persisted as he whipped off his sunglasses and shoved them into his shirt pocket. "I know this section of the road is pretty quiet. But I can't afford to take the chance. You know how much money it represents."

Clay shot her a black look. "I didn't hear anyone say you had to." With that he crouched to take the spare from the rack beneath his truck.

Willa understood then that he intended to loan her his spare tire and she felt her face flush with chagrin. "I really appreciate this," she said when he straightened and began rolling the tire to her pickup.

"I'm not doing it for you," he replied coldly, and Willa stiffened, scrambling to harden herself to his obvious dislike.

When they reached the back of her truck, she briskly took over, laboring to conceal her emotions as she loosened the lug nuts of the damaged tire before she positioned the jack and began to raise the truck. While she pumped the jack handle, Clay crouched once more and finished removing the tire. In no more than a few moments, the spare was in place and Clay was tightening the lugs.

"That wasn't the truth, Willa," he said suddenly, his voice going a little rough. He turned his head and looked at her, his dark eyes catching the shadows of hurt that lingered in her green gaze. "What I said just now about not doing this for you. It wasn't the truth."

Willa was suddenly overcome with sentiment, painfully aware that this small bit of tenderness from Clay was somehow much harder to take than his earlier show of disdain. She bent her head abruptly so he couldn't see the watery fullness that sprang to her eyes, as she made a project of lowering the jack, then pulling it from beneath the truck. Clay gave the lugs an extra turn before he straightened.

"Thanks, Clay," she managed, fighting to keep the huskiness from her voice as she avoided his gaze and reached for the lug wrench. By the time she'd returned it and the jack to their place behind the seat in the cab, Clay had opened the tailgate of the pickup and was about to load the first spool of wire.

They worked in silence until the wire was loaded and they'd got the trailer hitched to the truck. Willa retrieved the fence post she'd braced the trailer tires with while Clay hooked up the trailer lights and tossed the cement block back into the pickup. Willa was just about to climb into the cab, when Clay's fingers closed gently around her arm.

"About what happened in town today," he began, "I had nothing to do with it."

"I'd guessed that already. Thanks again for your help," she said, so deeply unnerved by his touch and by his unexpected change that all she wanted to do was flee. She forced a grateful curve to her lips and tried to look up at him, but her gaze went no higher than his shirt front. "I'll have your spare back to you as soon as possible."

As if he'd just become aware that he was touching her, he pulled his hand away. "Don't forget that hankie," he reminded her gruffly.

"I won't," she promised, then turned away from him to get into the truck.

"It's awfully damned hard to have you around here again, Willa," he said quietly, yet his candid admission communicated a gentleness that took her by surprise.

For just an instant, the years of estrangement fell away and Willa turned her head to look up fully into Clay's solemn countenance. Beneath his unconsciously intimidating look was an ache, a longing she recognized and understood. For a mere fraction of a second a familiar feeling of closeness surged between them. It was almost as if Angie had never died and Willa had never gone away.

Suddenly frightened that her own longings were blinding her to the hostility she should have been seeing, Willa sighed, then echoed grimly, "It's awfully damned hard to be here, Clay."

Willa stepped up into the truck and pulled the door closed, tugging off her gloves as she waited for Clay to stop staring at her and walk away. Just when she thought she couldn't bear another moment, Clay turned and started toward his truck. Willa hurriedly twisted the key in the ignition, then waited for Clay to back his vehicle out of the way.

She checked her mirror for traffic, then pulled slowly back onto the highway, the old pickup laboring under its load. She wasn't surprised when Clay turned his truck around and followed her past the turnoff to Orion. When she slowed, then got off the highway on the short road to the Circle H, the silver-and-black pickup stopped and managed an efficient three-point turn on the pavement to head back the other way.

CHAPTER FOUR

HER HAT BRIM SHADING HER FACE from the high midday sun, Willa drove the tractor and hay wagon beneath the wide second story door of the barn to begin the wearing process of levering the large bales of fragrant hay she'd collected from the hay field into the loft. The efficiency of the loft fork and pulley system made the job easier, but some assistance would have helped even more.

Willa thought instantly of Paige, who was up at the ranch house either reading a magazine or in the midst of her daily aerobic workout. Just having someone drive the tractor while Willa tossed the bales on the wagon would have been better than nothing, but Paige had resisted the idea all week, making excuses that ranged from not being good at driving a tractor to the negative effects of too much sun and wind on her complexion.

In addition to an aversion to outdoor work, Paige couldn't seem to manage to prepare a decent meal for the two of them. Paige could subsist on lettuce leaves and cottage cheese, but Willa needed something much more substantial to carry her through a dawn-to-dusk workday. It was no wonder Willa had grown frustrated and irritable this past week. TV dinners and cold sandwiches were not exactly the staples of good nutrition, but Willa rarely had the time or energy to fix herself something better.

That Paige didn't try to help her in even the smallest way only increased the animosity between the two cousins. Paige's too obvious scheme to discourage Willa into leaving was coming along so well that only with the utmost self-control was Willa able to conceal her discontent from Paige. She couldn't wait until she left for her next modeling assignment. With any luck it would be tomorrow, since the photo shoot had already been delayed a few days. Still, Willa cautioned herself not to count on anything until Paige was actually on the plane.

It had been a week since Willa had carted the wire and fencing home, yet she'd accomplished little but the most necessary fence repairs along with her daily checks on the cattle. The small hay pasture had needed to be mown and baled, and since Willa was forced to work the physically exhausting job alone, the other work around the ranch had fallen even further behind.

To top it all off, the two ranch hands she'd interviewed the day before had turned out to be unsatisfactory. One had a criminal record she was certain her aunt would be uncomfortable with. The other had seemed too much of a know-it-all, too often criticizing his past bosses for Willa to believe he'd make the type of loyal, dependable employee Aunt Tess needed.

There had been other calls that week in response to the ad, but only three would agree to come to an interview. It seemed that too many people knew about the problems on the Circle H and either were looking for something with a less shaky future or were hoping for better wages than Willa could promise. And, as much as she wished it weren't so, there were probably more than a few men who simply didn't want to work for Willa Ross, much less for a woman.

Willa finished putting up the hay, then started toward the house to grab a sandwich and exchange her coffee thermos for a larger one filled with ice water before she headed back to the hay pasture. She had just washed up and had set the water thermos in the kitchen sink to fill while she made a quick lunch, when she heard the sound of a vehicle coming up the driveway.

Clay Cantrell's pickup rolled past the house, stopping midway to the barn. Willa groaned as she recalled that although she'd had the tire fixed and replaced on her uncle's old truck, she hadn't got around to dropping Clay's spare off at Orion. She hurriedly slapped her sandwich together and left it on the kitchen counter to dash to the basement to get Clay's handkerchief from the ironing board.

She was just coming up the stairs, when she heard Paige's throaty voice.

"She's not much more competent than Art Boles," Paige was saying. "And I don't know what she does with her time, either. She doesn't have much to show for it except the bills she's been running up. I wish I could convince Mother to open her eyes, but you know how sentimental she is. I just hope Willa has an attack of conscience and doesn't hurt Mom too much this time. She just couldn't take it, Clay."

Willa's cheeks were burning with fury as she stepped into the kitchen and closed the door to the basement with quiet force. Paige was dressed in a lilac form-fitting exercise outfit that clung to her slim body like a second skin, and she was using it to advantage, having struck a pose calculated to look unconsciously seductive. Willa felt a sharp stab of something distressing like jealousy as she swiftly noted what a perfect physical match Paige's brunette looks were for Clay's imposing masculinity.

"You might know a bit more about how I spend my time if you could manage to get out of bed by noon," Willa remarked coolly as she crossed to where Paige and Clay stood just inside the back porch door. "Here's your hankie," she said to Clay, braving his disapproving expression as she held out the laundered, neatly pressed handkerchief for him to take. "If you'll give me a minute, I'll go get your spare." Willa turned away and got out some waxed paper to wrap her sandwich in as Paige led Clay toward the living room.

Doing her best to ignore the flirtatious note that came into her cousin's lowered voice as her words became indistinct, Willa selected fruit from the refrigerator and Twinkies from the bread box, then, along with her sandwich, placed them in a brown paper bag. Willa delayed a bit longer for a quick glass of cold milk before she added a handful of ice cubes to the thermos. She'd collected her lunch and the thermos and had carried it all back out to the hay wagon when Clay caught up with her.

"You've got a section of fence down and about fifty head of cattle out," he told her as she set the lunch sack and thermos on the tractor.

Willa was instantly alarmed. "Where?"

"On Orion."

Willa was unaware of the slight droop of her narrow shoulders as she glanced uneasily toward the cloud-mantled mountains miles to the west. "I've still got a lot of hay in the field, Clay, and it's supposed to storm tonight.''

Clay's voice was hard when he spoke. ''Your aunt hired you to run this ranch, Willa. If you can't handle it, maybe you ought to step aside.''

Willa's gaze swung back to his, her green eyes blazing as the effects of the heat, hard work and frustration of the past few days sent her temper skyward. ''If you think you can do as good with almost no money and no help, plus an overabundance of critics who are standing over you waiting for you to fail, you're welcome to try, Mr. Millionaire Rancher.'' She jabbed a slim finger at his chest angrily. ''Until then, either run those cattle back onto the Circle H and patch the fence yourself until I can get to it, or let them graze and send me the bill. I've got hay to get in.''

With that Willa turned her back on him and climbed onto the tractor. ''Your spare is in the pickup,'' she called over her shoulder as she started the engine and pulled away from the barn to head down the long twin tracks that led to the hay field.

WILLA WAS TOO EXHAUSTED and miserable to feel angry any longer at either Clay or her cousin as she trudged from the barn to the house that evening. Sweat-mingled hay chaff and dust had worked their way beneath her clothing all day and were now plastered to her skin by the downpour that had begun just as she'd driven the last wagon of hay from the field. The only dry comfortable place was inside her boots, but her feet were too sore for her to enjoy it.

At least the last wagon of hay had stayed dry, thanks to the tarpaulin she'd thrown over it just moments before the rain started. She'd pulled the hay wagon into the barn, resigned to unloading it in the morning so she could feed the horses and get up to the house for the brisk shower she hoped would pound away the scratchy hay chaff and revive her for the book work she needed to do before she made an early night of it.

The thought of spending a good share of the day tomorrow fixing fence and rounding up cattle was too tiring for her to contemplate, and she regretted now that she hadn't hired at least one of the men she'd decided was unsuitable. Willa made a mental note never to interview anyone after the kind of day she'd just put in. There was no telling what kind of person she'd get for her aunt if she gave in to desperation.

Thinking of Aunt Tess suddenly brought a pang of sadness. Willa hadn't had time to visit her much this week and it looked as if she wouldn't tonight, either. But that would have to change once Paige went on her assignment, since Tess would naturally miss her daughter's frequent visits. And since Tess was still struggling with her recovery and her grief over losing Cal, she'd need just that much more love and emotional support.

Willa didn't know what she'd do when her aunt was released from the hospital and sent home. She supposed she or Paige would have to see to hiring a nurse to look after Tess during the day while Willa was out working.

"And it would help a lot if that nurse could double as a housekeeper and cook," Willa said aloud to herself, then felt guilty for the selfish thought. Even though she was about to stare another TV dinner in the face—and wasn't certain whether she might rather prefer to go hungry—she had no right to consider anyone's comfort but her aunt's, since it was Tess's money that would be spent. Willa had the sudden idea as she reached the back porch and pried off her muddy boots that perhaps she should consider drawing on her personal bank account to hire a cook, but dismissed the idea. She was having enough trouble finding a foreman and a couple of ranch hands. In view of the way everyone in their small community felt about her, Willa doubted she'd find any woman in the area who would want to come in to cook and clean house for her.

Willa had stepped from the back porch into the kitchen and set the thermos on the counter, when she noticed the folded sheet of pink stationery propped up on the kitchen table. She walked over and picked it up, then heard the familiar sound of Clay's truck coming up the drive. She didn't have the energy to face a confrontation with him. Hurriedly, she skimmed the note her cousin had left informing her she'd gone to New York.

Relieved that Paige was finally gone, Willa tossed down the paper and quickly closed the back door. With any luck, she could get into the shower and pretend she didn't know Clay was there. Surely he'd leave if he got no response to his knock and couldn't find her down at the barn.

Moments later, Willa stepped beneath the sharp needles of hot water in the shower, lathering her hair twice before going after her skin with a shower brush and soap. She lingered under the hot spray, twisting the shower nozzle until the water pulsed down soothingly on her aching arms and shoulders. Too soon the water began to cool, and Willa reluctantly turned off the faucets and opened the shower door to reach for a towel.

After putting on the short terry robe she'd laid out, she quickly combed the wet tangles from her hair, then blow-dried it to a silky cloud of honey-brown that waved past her shoulders. Revived, but resigned to one of the frozen dinners waiting for her in the freezer and the load of book work she'd been putting off, Willa went downstairs, her bare feet soothed by the gentle abrasion of the rug on their tired soles.

Except for the kitchen, the house was darkened, the only other light coming through the windows from the yard and an occasional flash of lightning as the storm began to reintensify. Willa had just reached the doorway to the kitchen, when it registered that she hadn't turned on any lights downstairs when she'd come in.

"Hope you don't mind that I let myself in."

Clay's low drawl startled her as she stepped into the kitchen and saw him sprawled comfortably on one of the chairs at the table, a booted foot resting on his thigh, his Stetson upended on the cupboard near the back door.

"What are you doing here?" she demanded, her hand going automatically to the loose V of her robe as Clay's dark eyes made a slow journey downward. Willa caught her breath as Clay's gaze lingered first on the swell of her breasts, then on the slim length of thigh, knee and ankle that the short robe left uncovered. There was a pronounced glimmer of male appreciation in those midnight-black eyes before they shuttered themselves and returned to her face.

"I had one or two things I wanted to talk over with you tonight."

As she forced herself to recover from the heat that still lingered in the wake of that look, her lips thinned skeptically. "I'll just bet," she murmured, thinking of his criticism and Paige's when she'd come back to the house at midday. Willa crossed the room to the pantry and stepped around the corner to the large chest-style freezer. "I'm in no mood to hear any more about how incompetent I am or how many bills I'm running up," she called out to him as she started to rummage through the stack of boxed dinners.

"How old are you now, Willa, twenty-two?"

When she realized Clay was beside her, Willa straightened abruptly, hastily yanking down the short robe that had hiked up when she'd bent to look into the freezer. She flung an irritated glance at him and caught the unnerving blackness in his eyes as he forced his attention from her fully exposed leg to meet her gaze.

Several charged heartbeats of time thudded between them as green eyes melded with black. Clay was too close. The large pantry was suddenly dwarfed by his nearness, a nearness that pulsed with his rawly masculine presence and seemed to smother her with an odd lethargy.

As if the storm outside were somehow a barometer of the rising sensual voltage that arced between them, a long, slow-building rumble of thunder began, vibrating the kitchen windows and making itself felt as the floor beneath their feet began to tremble.

Neither of them moved or spoke as the thunder rolled steadily toward its crescendo, neither of them quite able to look away from the other as frail tendrils of feeling wove their way between them.

Willa suddenly remembered that time at Angie's birthday party when she'd managed to maneuver Clay away from their guests and lead him to the small stand of trees well past the stone patio at the Orion ranch house. She'd been sixteen, almost seventeen.

Over Aunt Tess's objection, Willa had bought a daring little ivory halter dress with a deep V neckline and no back for Angie's party with the secret intent of bringing home to Clay just how grown-up she was and how ladylike she could be.

She'd had a crush on him then, and since one or two of the schoolboys who'd been smitten with her had seemed to like kissing her, she'd decided the time had come to see if her kisses would have a similar effect on Clay.

Unfortunately the much older Clay Cantrell had made all the boys her age seem so green and shallow that she'd found kissing them not much of a thrill. Kissing Clay was to be a kind of experiment, an adventure. It had been deliciously dangerous to anticipate what it would be like to kiss a man like him, one who was so tall and strong, one who was so exciting to be around that she'd started to feel odd little flutters in the pit of her stomach whenever he was near.

Just like now, she realized hazily as the thunder grew deafening. But for those few small measures of time she was caught up more in her memory....

"I think this is far enough," Clay had said as he caught her hand and tugged her to a halt just past the first cluster of trees. There had been something quite intense about the way he'd looked at her then, something she'd seen only an inkling of before, and she'd felt both frightened and excited. When he didn't release her hand, but continued to hold it in the calloused warmth of his own, Willa had felt encouraged, almost confident, though she'd also felt alarmingly weak-kneed standing so close to him.

"You never asked me to dance tonight," she said breathlessly as she took that daring step nearer, practically forcing him to take her into his arms. When Clay obliged it seemed like the most natural thing in the world for her to reach up and place her hands on the back of his neck to draw him down those few inches.

Amazingly, magically, Clay's firm male mouth alighted gently on hers and Willa tried to kiss him as best she knew how, thoroughly shocked when Clay showed not even a hint of the enthusiasm her boyfriends had shown. When she drew back, Clay chuckled at her disappointed expression, and she felt insulted. Unable to bear the thought that Clay was laughing at her, she started to pull away, so furious that she almost struck him.

"Come back here, minx," he said in a low, rough voice as he pulled her back into his arms and held her slim resisting body against the male hardness of his. "You're too damned young to be seducing older men," he growled. "If you learn your lesson tonight, maybe you'll want to wait a couple more years before you try this again."

With that, he lowered his head and took her lips with a force that had almost made her faint. Indeed, she fairly melted beneath the sensual assault of his mouth. But when he pressed past her lips and invaded her mouth she became like a rag doll in his arms. When his mouth finally released hers she was too dazed to move, so overwhelmed that all she could do was cling weakly to him.

"Damned if I know which of us learned the lesson," she thought she heard him mutter, but she was too confused by the anger she sensed in him to be certain. He thrust her away from him and turned his back on her with a rough "You'd better get back to the party."

She did what he asked—for once—but had waited in abject misery for him to follow, so afraid that her foolishness had separated them forever that she'd almost gone home. But when he appeared a few minutes later, he acted as if nothing had happened, and she was so relieved that she'd never pulled another stunt like that—or wanted to—with anyone else again....

Willa recovered from the recollection and from somewhere found her voice. "W-what did you say?"

Clay didn't answer for a moment, and Willa felt the warm feeling of lethargy spread over her anew as he took another step toward her.

Suddenly she sensed that Clay was going to kiss her, and the realization was staggering.

But this time, he wouldn't be a man kissing a precocious teenager, she reminded herself dizzily. This time, he was a man about to kiss a woman he despised on every level, a woman whom he believed had caused his sister's death. Remembering that sobered her, and when she saw the tight anger that crossed Clay's features she knew he had remembered it, too.

The long, slow roll of thunder peaked with a crash, then ebbed into the loud drum of rain on the roof.

"How old are you, damn it?" he repeated, wrenching them both from those emotion-charged moments.

"What's that got to do with anything?" she hedged, sensing instantly what he was up to.

"Twenty-two?" he persisted.

"Twenty-two, going on eighty tonight," she said on an out-rush of weary breath as she turned and pulled the freezer door closed, banishing the last of the bittersweet memory as she concentrated on something more immediate. Perhaps the next few nights she'd eat at a restaurant in town on her way to the hospital to visit her aunt. But tonight she'd settle for a glass of milk and a peanut butter sandwich, suddenly put off by the thought of another frozen dinner.

"You've taken on a lot for someone your age," Clay pointed out a bit less sternly, but she could tell he was straining to be diplomatic.

Willa turned fully toward him, a wry twist to one corner of her mouth as she attempted to step around him. "Well, that's life, Clay," she said in a flippant tone meant to provoke. "It rarely waits until you're old enough or smart enough. Ready or not, here it comes." Willa moved past him, perversely letting her hip and thigh brush against his as she did so, though his swift intake of breath gave her much less satisfaction than she'd hoped.

"I assume you're trying to make a point," she said as she heard him follow her back into the kitchen. She pulled open the cupboard door where the peanut butter was kept, then set the jar on the counter next to the bread box before she got out a plate and butter knife.

"Paige said you turned down a couple of men who came out to apply for work. Was there something wrong with them, or were you just being too choosy?"

Clay's question revealed a world of suspicion. Nettled, Willa stepped aside and yanked open the refrigerator to get out milk and a jar of her aunt's home-made jelly.

"I explained to Paige why I didn't hire those men," she said as she set the milk and jelly on the counter next to the peanut butter and closed the refrigerator door. "No one would scream louder than she would if I'd hired either one of them. But," she added, flashing a sarcastic smile at him as she reached for a loaf of bread, "I'm sure she figured if she gave the truth just the right little twist she could have you over here making a nuisance of yourself."

Willa turned back to making her sandwich when Clay's expression darkened. "Both men's resumés are in on the desk in the den. Since you've obviously decided you're going to butt in on Circle H business, you might as well charge on in and see for yourself. It's pretty clear my word still means less than nothing to you."

Thick silence filled the room. Even the storm quieted for those next few seconds. Willa worked at her sandwich with jerky movements, her eyes blinded by the angry tears that had suddenly sluiced up from the old hurt inside.

She'd thought her friendship with Angie had included Clay, that the closeness and trust there'd been between the three of them had been unshakable. But Clay had never given her a chance to speak for herself after the accident; he'd already made up his mind. He'd believed Paige, a girl he hadn't known half as well as he'd known her, a girl who had no compunction about telling little white lies, one who'd often put just enough of a slant on the truth to get herself out of hot water, one who'd taken every possible advantage of a tragic situation, because Willa had been so close to death herself that Paige had initially believed she'd die, too, and that no one would ever find out who'd really been driving that day.

"Well, how about it, Clay?" she prodded, unable to calm her roiling emotions as an idea came to her. "While you're at it, you might as well look over the books and see how much money I've been bleeding out of the accounts. Come on." Willa tossed down the butter knife, wiped her hands on a dish towel, then stalked out of the kitchen and down the darkened hall to the den. She'd flung open the door and turned on every light in the room before she heard him walking down the hall after her.

Still stinging from the old betrayal, she got out the ranch ledgers, scooped up the bills and receipts she'd planned to tend to that night, then thumped them down in the middle of the desk as Clay stepped into the room. She spied the resumés on the corner of the desk and snatched them to add to the stack. When she looked up, she was trembling, but pride kept her from allowing anything to show but the anger she felt.

"Come on, let's get this over with," she invited irritably.

Clay's face was a stony mask. "That's not necessary."

"Oh, but it is," Willa said, straightening, her green eyes glittering. "I insist. It's time you learned to look at all the facts...and time someone called Paige's bluff." Willa reached out and gave the stack of ledgers and papers before her a little shove in his direction. "It's all here. Since yours is a surprise visit I haven't had time to alter any of the evidence."

When Clay still made no move to inspect the things she'd set out, Willa picked up the resumés and began reading them out loud, adding the impressions she'd formed during the interviews and her reasons for not hiring either man. Next she opened the ledgers and gave him a brief rundown of how much money there was in the accounts, before she began listing the expenses she'd incurred, as well as the ones she'd decided could wait.

"Added to that, I have no idea how much loss we'll show on the cattle, since the tallies at spring roundup were incomplete. Whoever was in charge missed branding—and I assume counting and vaccinating— several of the calves. Oh, I forgot," she went on acidly, "we've got only two good horses and we'll undoubtedly take another loss when the others go to auction and I have to buy replacements."

"That's enough," Clay said roughly just as she was about to add something else.

"Yes, that is enough. I agree," she said, pulling her robe a bit more snugly around herself and cinching the sash tighter around her small waist. "So you'll excuse me if I'm just a little slow getting things done or if it looks as if I'm spending my aunt into bankruptcy. As I told you before, I'll leave when I hire a couple of ranch hands and find someone competent to run the Circle H."

Clay was staring across the desk at her. He had finally stepped nearer to look at everything she'd laid out for him and Willa was certain at that moment that she hated him for needing a closer look at the evidence despite her invitation and his earlier protest.

"That's why I wanted to talk to you. I think I have a way to accomplish everything right away."

Willa watched him warily. "How?"

"Let me take over the search for a foreman and ranch hands. Until then, I can spare three or four of my men to come over and get things in order." Clay stopped, giving her a moment to consider.

Willa made the first objection that came to mind. "You can see from the books that I can't afford to pay wages for that many men."

"I'll be good for the wages. Paige already agreed to take care of supplies and operating expenses provided you leave the ranch."

Willa's lips twisted cynically. She should have known Paige was in on this.

"What about Aunt Tess?"

Clay misunderstood her question. "She won't know about the wages. Paige said Tess has made arrangements to stay with her friend Mabel Asner in town until she's strong enough to take care of herself. Everything should be finished by then."

Willa swallowed hard, her mouth dry as dust as she sensed Clay's eagerness to have her accept the proposal he and Paige had cooked up. That he was this close to Paige and was clearly involved with her made Willa feel slightly ill. But, then, she thought meanly, maybe he deserved to be hoodwinked by Paige.

"And if I go along with your idea, I could be gone by—let's say—tomorrow?" she offered, her light brows raised in question.

Clay's granite expression relaxed and he nodded, clearly relieved by her response.

"You know, don't you, that Aunt Tess has plans for me to stay on," she said, already guessing that neither he nor Paige had considered how Tess would feel about her leaving so soon. "Not that I intend to," she added when Clay's eyes hardened, "but tomorrow would be a bit too abrupt, don't you think?"

"How soon do you think it could be?" he shot back, and Willa was cut to her soul by his persistence—his obsession to banish her not only from his life, but from that of the only blood relative who would claim her.

The sadness she had managed to keep at bay most of the time began to overwhelm her and she shook her head, unable for a moment to speak. "You're pretty anxious to have me gone, aren't you?" she asked, forcing her voice to remain steady.

Clay stared at her a moment. "What do you think?"

"I think you must hate me an awful lot," she answered with soft candor.

Clay swore, his dark eyes suddenly glinting with pain-mingled anger. "Damn it all to hell, Willa, what do you expect?" he demanded, then exhaled irritably, running strong tanned fingers through his dark hair as he regained control of himself. In a more civilized voice he asked, "What about my proposal?"

Willa didn't answer right away as she struggled not to show how much his outright admission of hatred had hurt. Somehow she rallied, marshaling her pride, her manner as cold, aloof—as resolute—as she could manage.

"I'll think it over, but it's only fair to tell you that I want to stay—for Aunt Tess."

Clay's mouth slanted, and he looked away a moment as he shook his head. "I can't understand why you're doing this, Willa," he said, his voice laced with exasperation. "You and Paige are at each other's throats, half the town doesn't want to do business with you, and I'll bet you don't have one friend left around here, do you?"

Clay's gaze came back to hers challengingly, and when Willa didn't respond, he continued on, suddenly relentless. "You should have realized by now that when Tess asked you to stay on and help her, she was making more of an emotional request than a sound business decision. You're risking the loss of this ranch because you have some crazy idea that saving it is going to make up for other things. Other things," he said as his stern voice went somber, "that you can't atone for. I just hope you see sense before it goes too far."

"Is that all you have to say?" Willa asked brittlely.

"That's about it."

"Then I'd appreciate it if you'd leave," she said, managing to hold Clay's gaze without flinching until he turned from her and strode from the room. She listened to the muffled sound of his booted feet in the carpeted hall, listened when they reached the kitchen and thudded toward the porch door. The booted steps halted there and it was several moments before she heard the back door open, then close.

When it did, Willa sat down at the desk, the paperwork forgotten as a feeling of deep depression dragged her heart downward.

CHAPTER FIVE

THE WYOMING SKY was a bright blue, the storm clouds of three days before had long evaporated. The afternoon sun was hot, but the steady breeze that hummed through the stand of pines near Angela Cantrell's grave was cooling.

Willa had put off this visit to Angie's grave site for days—years, in fact. She'd been too severely injured in the accident to attend the funeral. When she'd recovered, she hadn't been able to come, either, as forbidden to do so by her own heart as by her uncle's order.

But now she was here, and the deep grief and sense of loss she still felt was amplified by the fact that today would have been Angie's twenty-third birthday. As Willa stopped at the foot of Angie's grave and stared at the brief lifespan indicated on the marble headstone, the heaviness in her chest grew unbearable as she whispered a soft "Hi, Ang."

Willa squeezed her eyes closed and the memory of Angie that she carried in her mind became unnaturally sharp. What she saw was a seventeen-year-old girl with dark, curly hair, merry brown eyes and coltishly long legs. Willa could still see the mischievous gleam in Angie's eyes and the ornery curve of her mouth as the two of them cooked up some piece of devilry—

usually directed at Clay because his good-natured retaliation could be counted on.

"I had to come here today," she whispered at last, easily picturing her best friend's quick smile of welcome. "It's been more than five years, and since it's your birthday..." Willa's voice trailed away as she looked down with tear-blurred eyes at the bouquet of miniature pink roses she held in a cone of florist's tissue. "I brought you these."

Willa stepped to the headstone and crouched down, removing the flowers from the tissue. Suddenly the sense of Angie's presence was so real that Willa half expected to see Angie leaning an elbow on the headstone, grinning down at her. The feeling was so remarkably strong that it was almost a shock not to see her friend standing there. A little unnerved, but comforted in an unexpected way, Willa felt her tension recede.

She lowered herself to the ground, sitting cross-legged at the side of the grave, any sense that she was trespassing gone. One by one, Willa separated the roses and leaned over to place them in the slim receptacle in front of the stone. When she was finished, she rested her elbows on her thighs and sat with her head bowed and her fingers combed deeply into her hair.

CLAY CANTRELL drove his truck beneath the scrolled iron arch that marked the entrance to the cemetery. As much as he'd wanted to ignore this anniversary, the melancholia he'd been feeling all day prevented it. Angie had loved parties and a good time and there was no way he could let her birthday go by without doing what little he could to remember it. It seemed that everything bright and fun had gone out of his life when Angie had died, and for the longest time, he'd thought the grieving would never stop. Eventually it had and he'd got over her death, but there were still times when those tender wounds were pricked. More so now that Willa was back. Just having her around had resurrected the pain, and suddenly this sentimental anniversary had once again become almost unbearable.

The moment Clay turned left at the fork of the one lane road that led to the far end of the cemetery, he saw Willa's car. His mouth tightened grimly as he glanced beyond it toward the hill and the cluster of pines that stood between the road and the Cantrell family plot. That Willa would visit Angie's grave angered him and as he drew his truck to a halt behind her car, he vowed to do something about it.

"I'M SO SORRY, Ang," Willa whispered, her forehead in her hands as the tears finally broke. "I wasn't strong enough. Maybe you were already... gone... before I could get to you." Willa paused, fighting to keep the worst of the memory repressed. "I guess I'll never know for sure." For several minutes, tears of that remembered agony slid in a torrent down her cheeks. At last she raised her head and looked again at the name on the headstone, Angela Elaine Cantrell, and the birth and death dates just seventeen years apart.

The tears continued, but as the sense of uncomforted grief finally eased, Willa slowly began to feel better. Coming here had been a release, a chance to talk things over with an old friend, a time to ask for forgiveness and find it. As crazy as it seemed, Willa somehow knew now that Angie wouldn't have thought she'd done anything that needed to be forgiven. And though realizing that didn't lessen Willa's sense of responsibility, she felt more at peace than she had for years.

Willa drew a shaky breath, unaware of the harsh-faced man who stood only a few feet behind her. "I still miss you, Ang."

The scuff of a boot in the grass startled her. As she jerked her head around, she saw Clay's denim-clad legs and her eyes shot up to his iron countenance.

Clay stared down at Willa's tear-ravaged face. He'd been prepared to rail at her, to challenge her right to be here, but the instant he'd heard her emotion-clogged voice and listened to the things she was saying to Angie—just as if Angie were sitting there with her—something inside him had started twisting.

She was turning him inside out, forcing him to feel things he wanted to ignore, deepening the conflict within him that tore open old wounds and inflicted new ones. He had softened toward Willa considerably in the three weeks she'd been here, and he hated himself for it. It wasn't right that Willa had survived the foolishness that had taken his kid sister's life. Everything good and compassionate and gentle that Willa aroused in him somehow seemed disloyal to Angie.

As he watched Willa scramble to her feet and turn fully toward him, Clay couldn't prevent his gaze from wandering downward, his mind suddenly filled with the sensuous memory of how she'd looked in that short robe the other night.

Warily Willa watched the changing emotions that crossed Clay's face. Apprehension filled her when his fingers tightened punishingly on the stems of the white lilies he held at his side. Yet when his gaze came back to meet hers, it was bleak, the shafts of pain she read there bringing a fresh sting of tears.

Neither of them said a word as Willa picked up the crumpled florist's tissue and stepped past Clay to hurry to her car.

WILLA JABBED the slender spade into the gap between the fence post and the edge of the post hole, tamping down the dirt to wedge the new post more firmly into place. At midmorning, the hot June sun was already scorching through her clothing, but Willa felt oblivious to it. She was thinking only of the call she'd made to Clay the night before.

"I've thought about your offer," she'd told him as evenly as she could, determined to hide the emotional turmoil that had plagued her in the two days since she'd seen him at the cemetery. "And I was wondering if you'd consider a compromise."

At Clay's gruff "What is it?" Willa tentatively accepted the offer he'd made to find a foreman and a couple of ranch hands for the Circle H—but on the condition that she have final approval of who was hired.

Silence followed her counterproposal, but the instant objection she'd expected never came. When Clay reminded her about the other part of his proposal— that he send over some of his men to work on the Circle H—she'd accepted.

"But until you find a foreman, I'd like to stay on and keep working. There's more than enough to go around," she added, then waited for what felt like an eternity before Clay spoke.

"Paige's condition for providing the money for expenses was that you leave the ranch," he reminded her, and Willa felt herself wilt a little at his outspoken determination to have her go.

She had pressed a shaky hand against her forehead, grateful that she'd called Clay rather than gone to see him face to face. "I've just looked over the accounts. There's enough money to cover the outstanding expenses and supplies if I'm careful. I've kept a good record, so Paige can reimburse the accounts after I'm gone. Besides, it might take you a while to find a foreman."

Clay said nothing for so long that she thought they'd been disconnected. Resentment shot through her.

"I realize you and Paige are counting the minutes until I'm out of your lives forever," she said to break the silence, unable to keep the sarcastic edge from her voice, "but Aunt Tess doesn't feel that way, and she wouldn't understand if I suddenly turned everything over to you and disappeared."

A soft curse came over the line and Willa's temper flared. "If you decide you can live with my counter-proposal, you can send over a couple men to help me replace that section of fence that borders Orion. If you can spare more than two, I could use someone else to ride fence and check on the cattle in the south section along the highway." Willa took a quick breath. "Tell your men to pack their own lunches if they expect to eat. I'll be starting on the fence at seven." She hung up the phone before Clay could agree or not.

When she'd arrived at the fence line that morning just before seven with the wire and fence posts needed to do the job, two of Clay's men were waiting for her.

"I'm Frank Casey, and this here's Bill Johnson," Frank offered, and both men touched their hat brims in a show of politeness. "The boss sent us over to give you a hand."

Willa could detect nothing but respect in the manner of the two ranch hands and felt her mouth move into a reserved smile. "I appreciate your help."

The three of them had got right to work, removing several lengths of rusted, brittle wire to prepare for the new. Next they began digging up a few old rotted posts along this stretch of fence, replacing them with sturdy new ones. By that night, the new wire would be up and the most extensive of the repairs on this section would be made.

But Willa's relief at getting the job done and being spared the frustration and exhaustion of doing it alone was marred by the regret she felt. She should have been more considerate of Clay's feelings, more tolerant of his wish to have her gone, when they'd spoken on the phone the night before. Several times since she'd seen him at the cemetery, she'd relived those brief moments when she'd seen the pain on his face and the bleak look in his eyes.

Finding her at Angie's grave had obviously upset him, and in spite of how he felt about her, she hated causing him more pain. Although she'd felt as justifiably angry as when they'd talked on the phone, she should have made the extra effort to be a bit more patient, more diplomatic. In view of the fact that Clay thought her responsible for Angie's death, he was behaving with remarkable tolerance. Willa wasn't certain she'd be able to treat him as well if their situations were reversed. Some kind of apology was in order, though she wasn't quite sure how to make it without stirring everything up again.

As Willa finished with the fence post and moved down her part of the row to the next, she caught sight of Clay's silver-and-black pickup as it crested the hill on the Orion side and drove over the rough pasture toward her and the men.

Apprehensive suddenly, Willa made a project of using the slim shovel to rake loose dirt from the old post hole in preparation for the new post. Clay was probably here to speak to his men, so it was possible there would never be a private moment for her to say anything to him, much less voice an apology.

When Clay stepped out of his truck, Willa looked up from her work, but could read nothing in the hard black gaze that swung toward hers, then veered away as if he were ignoring her.

Willa worked on, listening to the easy sound of male voices as Clay joined his men, though she couldn't quite make out what was being said. The talking continued as she reached for the post-hole digger to deepen the hole.

Impatient, hoping yet dreading that Clay would come her way, Willa glanced toward him again, catching his eyes on her as he started in her direction. Hastily lifting a last bit of dirt from the post hole, Willa finished with the digger.

"I sent one of my men to check on the cattle," Clay said, the stony expression beneath his hat brim quite different from the one he'd just shown his men.

"Thanks," she murmured, her gloved hands gripping the digger handles nervously. Clay nodded, then started to turn toward his truck. Now was the time to say something to him about the night before. It might make no difference in how he felt toward her, but her conscience would be eased, and at least she could say she'd made the attempt. "Wait. There's something I need to say." Willa watched the stern, unfriendly set of Clay's face for any sign of softening when he turned back to her.

"I shouldn't have lost my temper last night," she said on an out-rush of breath. "I can understand how anxious you are to have me gone, and I'm sure I'd feel the same way if things were the other way around...." Willa could no longer meet the hard gleam in his eyes and her gaze slid from his. "Under the circumstances, you've been more than tolerant with me, and I want you to know that I'm sorry my being here is...hard on you," she got out, remembering how he'd told her that day along the highway that having her around again was hard, "damned hard," as he'd put it. "I plan to have the talk with Aunt Tess that I should have had days ago. That way, she'll have as much time as possible to get used to the idea. I'll be ready to leave as soon as you find a foreman."

Willa glanced away, looking off into the distance, feeling awkward and more than a little sad, though she was careful not to let it show on her face. That Clay was sensitive enough to her changing emotions to see it anyway would not have occurred to her.

"I've got a man in mind who might make a good foreman for your aunt."

Willa's gaze shot back to Clay's as he went on. "I gave him a call this morning. He's the assistant foreman on a big ranch up by Sheridan. He's good with horses, knows cattle, and he's been thinking about finding a smaller operation closer to his sister and her family in Laramie. The Circle H might be just what he's looking for.''

Willa tried not to show her surprise. Clay was evidently confident about the man.

''I'd appreciate a chance to talk to him myself before any decisions are made,'' she said firmly.

A look of impatience crossed Clay's face. ''I want this over with as soon as possible, Willa,'' he grumbled irritably. ''Don't make excuses to keep it going.''

''We have an agreement,'' she reminded him stiffly.

''Some agreement,'' he growled. ''After you got done with it, it wasn't much of a deal, was it?''

Willa's chin went up slightly. ''But you accepted it, or your men wouldn't be over here this morning,'' she pointed out.

Clay stared down at her, his dark eyes holding hers with a glimmer that was startlingly cold. ''I'd probably agree to just about anything that got you away from here and out of our lives for good.''

Willa felt herself go pale as she reeled inwardly from the impact of Clay's words. Her gaze was obscured by the abrupt dip of her hat brim as she looked downward. ''I've got work to do,'' she murmured as she focused on the tight grip she had on the post-hole digger.

Clay didn't linger. Turning his back, he walked away from her and her eyes crept upward to watch him go. His stride was angry and swift. He ignored his men as he crossed to the Orion side of the fence line and climbed into his truck.

With her vision beginning to blur with tears, Willa turned and tossed down the digger, not seeing that the tip of one handle came down sharply next to a long patterned shape that wiggled between a roll of new wire and the fence post she was about to pick up. The warning rattle of the snake didn't sound until her gloved hands closed around the post.

CHAPTER SIX

WILLA GASPED and instinctively jerked away from the sharp pain in her left wrist, horrified to realize she'd been bitten by a rattlesnake. The sound of the rattle, the strike, the pain—it all happened so quickly she hadn't had time to avoid it. Willa watched, dazed with disbelief, as the snake slithered away into the rough grass and disappeared.

Revulsion brought instant nausea as she caught the musky scent the agitated rattlesnake left in its wake. Willa shucked her work gloves and let them drop to the ground, then unbuttoned her shirt cuff and wrenched it up to reveal the twin puncture wounds of the bite.

Clay had just climbed into his truck and was about to start the engine, when he saw Willa drop her gloves and yank her sleeve up. Though her back was toward him, he sensed instantly that something was wrong. Irritated that everything within him was suddenly alert, he watched a moment more.

Willa glanced anxiously in Clay's direction, relieved to see he wasn't driving away, until she remembered what he'd just said to her. *I'd probably agree to just about anything that got you away from here and out of our lives for good.*

The strong pulse of pain in the area of the bite reclaimed Willa's attention and she saw that her wrist was already beginning to swell. Though she'd hoped no venom had been injected into the bite wounds—she knew that happened sometimes, a "dry bite," it was called—the onset of swelling and sharper pain told her she hadn't been so lucky. Panicked at the thought that she was in a potentially life-threatening situation, and that she was as good as alone, Willa started swiftly toward the Circle H pickup.

Calm down, she cautioned herself as she slowed her pace. The worst thing she could do now was give in to the hysteria that threatened to claim her. Still, as foolhardy as it was, she found she was practically running to the truck, her relief at reaching it squelched when she got the passenger door open and dug into the glove compartment for the snake bite kit that should have been there, but wasn't.

"Willa?"

Willa heard Clay's shout and turned her head to see that he had just stepped out of his truck and was waiting for a response from her. Tamping down her terrible longing for his presence and his help, Willa waved him away, then leaned farther into the truck to rummage beneath the seat for the kit.

She didn't need anyone, she reminded herself. She'd got along for a long time alone. She'd survived, but until that awful moment she hadn't realized how deep and how keen the estrangement she'd suffered had gone. There was nothing but loneliness and fear deep down inside her—fear of getting too close to anyone, fear of rejection, fear of intimacy....

Willa shoved those distressing thoughts aside as her fingers closed around the plastic box she'd been searching for. Trembling with haste, she pulled it from beneath the seat and worked at the stubborn catch.

"Willa, what the hell—"

Clay's voice startled her just as she got the kit open, and the contents spilled to the floor. She grabbed wildly for them, the desperation she felt making her clumsy.

"Haven't you got anything better to do?" she snapped, trying her best to conceal what she was doing from Clay. There should be plenty of time to administer the proper first aid and then drive herself to the hospital in Cascade.

"Let's see," Clay ordered as he took hold of her arm to turn her toward him. Willa winced at the fresh stab of pain, but didn't cry out.

"Damn it, Willa," he growled, then shouted for his men. Frank and Bill stopped working immediately and hurried over.

"I'll be all right," Willa told him as she tried to pull away. "I can take care of it myself."

Clay ignored her resistance and quickly inspected the puncture wounds and the swelling beneath. He released her only long enough to lift her to the truck seat. By then Frank and Bill had reached them.

"Snakebite," he told them as he forced Willa's sleeve high enough to apply a tourniquet. "One of you'd better use the CB to call someone at the house. Have them notify the hospital so they can be ready. And we'd better have a look at the size of the snake."

"It's gone," Willa cut in.

"Have a look around, anyway," Clay directed. As his men hurried away, Clay finished tying the constricting band just above her left elbow—tight enough to impede the flow of venom through the lymph system in her arm, but not tight enough to slow the artery.

"I can do the rest," Willa insisted, and as Clay reached for the antiseptic she pulled away from him.

"Damn it, Willa, this is serious," he growled as he swiftly reclaimed her arm and spilled some antiseptic over the wounds.

"But very convenient for you and Paige, wouldn't you say?" she shot back, barely noticing the sting of the antiseptic.

"What's that supposed to mean?" he demanded, then used his teeth to rip open the cellophane that held the sterile razor as he positioned Willa's wrist to make the quarter inch incisions through the puncture wounds that would allow the venom to drain.

"You know what I'm talking about," she told him, her voice low and trembling with more emotion than she could control. "You and Paige have been so eager to get rid of me..."

Clay's midnight eyes flashed angrily to hers for an instant before he looked down again to make the shallow cuts. "Not this way, Willa. Neither of us wants it this way and you know it." Clay reached for the suction and applied it to the fang marks.

"Oh, yeah?" she challenged, feeling nauseous and a little faint as the pain in her arm increased.

Clay raised his hand and grasped her chin to stare intently into her eyes. "Yeah," he answered, his voice rough and harsh. "And I don't ever want to hear that from you again." He didn't release her and she couldn't escape the look of anger in his eyes, which changed instantly to a look of tender concern. "You aren't feeling so good right now, are you?"

"I'm all right," she said with stiff dignity, not wanting to let Clay see that she was frightened and beginning to feel worse.

"It's going to be a rough ride out of here," he said as he released her chin to slide his calloused palm along her jaw and cheek. The soothing caress surprised her, but even more so when she realized Clay's hand was shaking.

"We don't have much choice, do we?" she asked, then saw something flare to life in Clay's eyes. He chaffed his palm gently against her cheek and slowly shook his head.

"No," he said, his voice a low rasp that moved over the surface of her emotions like rough velvet. "No choice at all, I guess."

WILLA LAY fully dressed on the hospital bed, staring at the television positioned on the wall across the room as she waited for the chaplain to stop by and give her a ride to the Circle H. It had been almost a day and a half since Clay had carried her into the emergency room and turned her over to the doctor's care. Nurses and technicians had come at her from all directions, bathing the bite area, taking blood samples, doing periodic checks of her vital signs, taking her medical history and getting an account of the bite. The antivenin had been administered quickly and successfully, but because there was the chance she'd need more, she'd been admitted to the hospital and given a private room.

Clay had stepped into the treatment area to see her before she'd been taken upstairs, but he'd stayed only long enough to learn that she was doing well and that she would need to stay in the hospital at least twenty-four hours. She hadn't seen him since.

Willa pressed the remote button that switched off the television, thoroughly weary of daytime programming. She'd needed a distraction from the unpleasant memories that had been triggered by her brief hospital stay, but television hadn't supplied it. Ever more restless, she glanced over at the wall clock, then got up, impatient to see that it was just after five. The chaplain had promised to be there by four, so Willa had already taken care of checking out.

She'd just started to make a call to his office, when the door to her room swung open. Thinking it was the chaplain, Willa quickly hung up the phone and turned around. "I was just—" Her smile of welcome faltered as Clay walked into the room, the overnight case she'd brought with her to Cascade in his hand.

"Feeling better?"

Clay stopped near the foot of the hospital bed, rotating the Stetson slightly on his fingers as his gaze swept over her. Willa struggled against the strong emotion that gripped her at the sight of him, amazed that he had this kind of effect on her. He seemed taller than ever suddenly, overwhelmingly male, and it was all Willa could do to keep her eyes from straying over his broad-shouldered, lean-hipped height.

"Feeling good enough to go home," she said a bit nervously. "As soon as Reverend Collins gets here."

"I spoke to him earlier," Clay informed her. "If you don't mind, I'll give you that ride back to the Circle H." Before Willa could respond, Clay held the small case out to her. "I thought you'd like to stop in and see Tess first, so I picked up a change of clothes for you."

Willa looked up from the case to Clay, taken aback by the personal intrusion into her life that his actions represented. If he'd truly brought her a change of clothes, that meant that he'd been in her room at the ranch and had gone through her belongings to get them. The thought gave her an odd feeling.

"That was...nice of you," she said awkwardly, then reached for the case. "I'll just be a minute."

Willa changed quickly in the room's private bath, pleased that she didn't have to wear her soiled work clothing home, but a bit pink cheeked to see that Clay had also chosen a set of her laciest underwear. The white jeans he'd selected were fine for a summer evening, and the long loose sleeves of the lime blouse would easily conceal her bandaged wrist from her aunt. He'd even thought to include a few cosmetics—just what she normally would have worn for the visit—and Willa applied them with a light hand.

"I really appreciate this, Clay," she said when she'd stepped out of the bathroom. "Aunt Tess might have worried if I hadn't stopped by again tonight."

Clay took the small bag from her. "I assumed Tess hadn't been told," he said, then gestured for her to precede him from the room.

Clay left the overnight case at the nurses' station on the floor Tess was on, then went with Willa to Tess's room. Willa was surprised Clay was going in with her, but she didn't question him. She felt unusually tired, in spite of spending most of the day resting, and although she was eager to see her aunt, she was just as eager to get the visit over with so she could go home.

"Willa!" Tess glanced past her visitor the moment Willa walked in, her instant smile widening when she caught sight of Clay. "And Clay!" she added, pleased. Willa crossed to the side of the bed opposite from where Mabel Asner stood, and leaned over to kiss her aunt's cheek.

Clay took a place at the foot of the bed, one corner of his mouth hitching up in carefully suppressed amusement when he saw the surprise on Mabel's ruddy face as she glanced from Willa to him. "Evening, Tess. Mabel."

"Are you two together?" Mabel asked, clearly bursting with curiosity.

"Willa and I are having dinner together tonight," Clay answered smoothly, and Willa felt herself reel in shock. If she hadn't sensed earlier that something between them was different, she did now.

"How are you today, Aunt Tess?" Willa asked casually to hide her confusion. The conversation settled quickly into what the doctor had said that day and who'd been by. And thanks to Mabel, Willa and Clay also got to hear the latest bit of gossip about each of Tess's visitors.

"I'm afraid Mabel missed her calling," Clay remarked as they walked to where he'd parked his car. "She should have been a news hound for some big city newspaper. Or leastways a gossip columnist somewhere."

Willa's mouth formed a bitter line. She was unable to see much that was humorous about Mabel's penchant for gossip since she'd been a victim of it. "Then why did you tell her we were having dinner together? A piece of news like that will get all over the county in less than a half hour," she said, then added crossly, "you started something you definitely won't appreciate tomorrow."

Clay escorted her to the passenger door and opened it for her before he spoke. "You need to eat, don't you?" he asked. He closed the door before she could respond. When he'd got her case into the trunk and eased his long body onto the seat beside her, Willa was watching him mistrustfully.

"What's come over you?" she demanded to know. "Why are you doing all this?"

Clay flashed a look in her direction that skittered away as his face hardened slightly. He pushed the key into the ignition and gave it a twist. "Let's don't ask too many questions right now," he said, his voice curt and tinged with just a trace of the unfriendliness she'd come to know all too well. "Why don't we just relax and see how things go from here?"

Willa stared at him as he backed the car smoothly from the parking space, then studied his flinty profile as he drove out of the lot.

"You feel guilty about what you said yesterday," she concluded with a cynical twist of lips.

When Clay didn't have a quick answer, Willa sighed, struggling to push away all the emotions he was so carelessly arousing. She had to clarify the situation for them both.

"Look, if I'd been paying attention to what I was doing, I wouldn't have got bitten by a snake," she reasoned. "If I hadn't been bitten, you wouldn't have had an attack of conscience. I'd probably be out fixing fence right now, and you'd still be pressing me to leave Cascade."

Clay made no response to what she'd said, and Willa went tense as he turned down a familiar street and pulled into the parking lot of the Silver Spur restaurant.

"I'm not really up to this," Willa said quickly as Clay reached up to switch off the engine. Willa's green eyes had gone shadowy and the turbulence in them communicated more fear than anger. "I mean it, Clay."

Clay studied her face for a long moment before he looked away and put the car into gear. The entire ride to the Circle H passed in silence.

"Thanks for the ride—for everything," Willa said as Clay brought the car to a smooth stop in the drive. She wasted no time in levering open her door to step out. As she walked to the back of the car for her overnight case, Willa tried to conceal the weariness that was creeping over her. When Clay got out and unlocked the trunk, Willa reached for her case, but he took it for her.

"I can get that," she said as he closed the trunk, but Clay shook his head and walked with her to the back porch door. To Willa's surprise, he carried her case all the way into the kitchen and set it on the floor.

"Is there anything you need?" he asked. The sudden awkwardness between them somehow felt unnatural even though they were enemies of sorts.

"No. Nothing."

"Then I'll head on down to the barn and take care of a few chores before I go."

"I think I can handle that much," Willa told him, uncomfortable with all his help.

"You should be resting."

Anxiety flickered through her and she was suddenly frightened of mistaking any of this for genuine caring or friendship on Clay's part.

"Don't, Clay."

Her soft plea smoothed out some of the harsher angles of his face and gentled the look in his eyes. "I'll see to those chores," he insisted gruffly, then turned and walked out the back door.

Willa watched him go, then glanced around the kitchen. Any appetite she had was gone. Unusually weary, her legs leaden with fatigue and unhappiness, Willa headed for the sofa in the living room.

THE NIGHTMARE WAS the same as always—more flashback than dream—so vivid and so eerily real that it was like being wrenched from the present. Each time it managed to escape her subconscious and invade her sleep-fogged mind, Willa relived every agonizing detail of what had happened that warm spring afternoon when Angie had died.

"God, Willa, you drive like an old woman," Paige was saying as she impatiently thrust a dark skein of hair behind her shoulder. Willa had started out from the stop sign after coming to a full stop and looking both ways, but because Paige was in a hurry to get home, Willa's caution aggravated her.

Angie, who was sitting between the two cousins, elbowed Willa, and Willa momentarily turned her head and grinned at her friend, then glanced past her to a sulking Paige, who had propped an arm on the open window and was drumming her fingernails impatiently on the roof of the pickup.

Willa and Angie had taken Uncle Cal's new truck to town to pick Paige up from a friend's house, but it was Saturday, and Paige had a hot date that night with a college boy home on spring break. Paige had been a bit too full of herself all week, more bossy and conceited than usual, so naturally Willa and Angie had taken it upon themselves to have a bit of harmless fun with her. As far as they were concerned, Paige was long overdue.

Willa continued to obey the speed limit a bit more faithfully than she might have otherwise, and she and Angie shared a secret grin or two when Paige continued to squirm and complain.

Just before they reached the edge of town, Angie started to cough. "Gosh, Willa," she said after the spasm of coughing had subsided, "I could sure use something to drink." Willa had easily perceived the dry hack as a put-on and quickly took her cue.

"Me, too," she'd chimed in, then flipped on the signal to turn at the next corner.

"You can wait till you get home," Paige snapped, then crossed her arms sullenly across her chest when Willa ignored her and made the turn that would take them to a convenience store. By the time Willa pulled into the store parking lot, Paige was fuming.

"Can we get you something, Paige?" Willa had asked solicitously, seemingly oblivious to Paige's pique.

"Just hurry up," Paige said through gritted teeth, but Angie found a way to dawdle as she started counting out the change in her pocket and made a production of trying to figure if she would have enough left over for a candy bar or only a pack of gum.

By the time Willa and Angie had finally gone in to make their selections and had come back out, Paige was behind the wheel. Figuring Paige had had enough, the other two girls climbed docilely into the truck, Angie choosing the middle of the long bench seat and Willa taking the place by the door.

Provoked and in a hurry, Paige had roared out of the parking lot, ignoring speed limit and traffic signs in an attempt to make up for lost time. It crossed Willa's mind to suggest that they all put on their seat belts, but a sudden dip in the road caused her to spill her soda down the front of her shirt and she'd forgotten about the safety precaution.

A few minutes later, on the graveled back road Paige had chosen as a short cut, the truck hit a series of washboard bumps and Paige lost control....

Willa awakened to blinding pain in her head and the strong, sickening fumes of gasoline. The truck lay upside down in the ravine a few feet from her and Willa moved instinctively toward it.

At first, the pain in her shoulder and arm was too great for her to crawl. Each breath she took brought a stabbing pain to her side that dimmed her vision. Slowly, agonizingly, she managed to use her other arm to pull herself along, the effort making her dizzy and nauseous. Paige, she'd noticed, was lying on the bank just above and behind the overturned truck, but Angie was nowhere in sight.

Wave upon wave of sickening fear washed through her, compelling her to get to Angie. From somewhere it registered that the gas tank had ruptured and that fire was imminent. Sobbing, struggling, fighting back the black void that tried to claim her, Willa clawed her way to the truck, the sight she saw in the wreckage of the overturned vehicle bringing with it a cry of horror.

CLAY HEARD the odd, softly keening wail just as he was about to get into his car. Sensing something was wrong when he heard the strange sound a second time, he shut the door, then hurried toward the house. Hesitating on the porch steps, he recognized Willa's voice.

Fear gripped him as he wrenched open the door, then ran toward the sounds.

Willa lay on the sofa, a knee upraised as her head moved fitfully from side to side, caught up in the nightmare that had left her drenched with perspiration. Clay froze in the doorway as she again made the wailing, whimpering sound he'd heard.

"Angie, wake up."

Clay listened intently, recognizing Angie's name from the mumbled syllables. He stared a moment, too stunned to move as he watched Willa struggle with the nightmare as if she were searching for something, reaching.

"Please, Angie, wake up."

A shudder coursed through his body and landed like a fist in his chest as he recognized the words and heard the utter desperation in Willa's voice.

CHAPTER SEVEN

THE HANDS THAT GRIPPED her upper arms and shook her awake were unlike the ones that had pulled her away from the wreckage just before the truck burst into flames, but Willa fought them as she'd fought those other hands. She had to save Angie. She couldn't let herself be pulled away before she could get Angie out.

"No. No, don't. Angie's in there," she babbled wildly, then found herself sitting up, her fingers dug like claws into Clay's shoulders.

Willa stared, eyes rounded in shock as nightmare and reality clashed.

"Angie? Did she—" The nightmare dimmed and receded, leaving in its wake a soul-deep feeling of grief and terrible loss. "Oh, God," she whispered raggedly, squeezing her eyes closed as she bowed her head, her breath coming in great gasps as the sobs rose in her chest like fire.

Clay couldn't take his eyes from her stricken face. The desolation he saw there clutched at him and drew him in as the shock of what he'd just heard pulsed through him.

He realized then what he should have realized five years before—that Willa hadn't intended for anyone to be hurt. The accident had to have been the result of a crazy adolescent stunt that had gone tragically wrong. It occurred to him suddenly that it could just as easily have been Angie who'd taken that reckless chance. The tenderness that welled up inside him as he continued to hold Willa drained the last of his hostility.

"Please, just leave me alone," she said hoarsely as she shoved him away, then shifted to the end of the sofa. Too overwrought to sit still, Willa got unsteadily to her feet and walked to the west windows of the living room to stare out despairingly at the purpling sunset of the waning day. The play of long shadows mingled eerily with the lingering effects of the nightmare and Willa wrapped her arms around herself, aware of the ache in her wrist and arm as she began to shiver.

"Are you all right?"

Willa went a little more rigid as she kept her back to him and tried to control the maelstrom of emotion that roiled inside her. The nightmare hadn't come this hard for months.

"Willa?" The deep velvety texture of Clay's voice and the undisguised concern it betrayed sent more tears flooding down her cheeks.

"I'm all right," she said briskly, then brought both hands up to brush impatiently at the wetness on her face. "You did the chores?" she asked, forcing her voice to sound steady and normal.

"Forget the chores," Clay said gruffly as he came to his feet and crossed the room. Willa stiffened as Clay stopped inches from her. "Do you have nightmares about Angie often?"

Willa bit her lip to stifle the sob that welled up in answer. The silence that stretched out was as thick and smothering as the black dreams that still hovered somewhere in the dark corners of her mind. Willa couldn't bear to have Clay pry into any of them, but she couldn't seem to form the right words to tell him so.

"Go away," she got out at last, then began to tremble as Clay's big hands came up and settled consolingly on her shoulders. She made a move to step away, but his fingers tightened, then began a soothing massage that radiated a warmth through her body that worked at the cold quivering knot deep inside. He stepped even closer as she began to shake, the heated impact of his nearness making her want to lean back and meld with his strength.

"Please. Just go away," she whispered hoarsely, her breathing fast and erratic as she tried to keep from turning and throwing her arms around him to grab for every bit of comfort his actions hinted at.

Clay felt the emotional tug of war within Willa only because the war of emotions within himself had been so acute. Compassion filled his heart.

"Not just yet, Willa," he said quietly, then turned her toward him and took her into his arms.

Willa clung to Clay helplessly, unable to resist the comfort she'd had so little of after the trauma of Angie's death and the terrible estrangement that had followed. No one had seemed to give much thought to the shock and desolation she'd felt at her friend's sudden death and the horrible manner in which she'd died. Even Aunt Tess had seemed distant and uncaring then.

"It's all right, Willa. It's all over," Clay soothed as he held her trembling body and let her cry. She felt as fragile as a small child in his arms and Clay couldn't help the protectiveness he felt toward her as he gathered her closer and led her to the large rocking chair beside the windows.

Willa's soft, pliant body molded easily to the solid planes of his as he pulled her down onto his lap and began to rock her like a baby. With the gentlest of hands he stroked her hair as her grip on him became frantic and the tears came hotter and harder.

It was some time later, when the room had gone completely dark, that the tears finally stopped. Willa rested weakly against Clay, her cheek on his damp shoulder as she listened to the steady rock of the chair and felt the calming rhythm of it to her soul. Clay's arms were still tight around her and Willa savored the security of his closeness, wondering at the meaning of it.

"Angie had her share of nightmares when she was little," Clay began, his deep voice a pleasant rumble against her chest. "Her favorite cure was the rocking chair." Clay continued to rock, raising his hand to stroke Willa's cheek.

At the mention of Angie's name, Willa went tense. Clay brushed his fingers over Willa's hair and softly ordered her to relax.

"She was my best friend, Clay," Willa whispered, the tremor in her voice a remnant of the emotional upheaval she'd just weathered. "I wouldn't have put her life in danger for anything in the world." Behind her words was the plea for Clay to at last believe this, to at last believe she hadn't caused the accident that had killed his sister. She couldn't tell him the truth outright because it would devastate Aunt Tess, yet she couldn't help but hope he would somehow realize it anyway.

Clay lowered his hand to rub her arm. "I know, Willa," he said huskily, and her heart gave a glad leap. She pressed against his chest to sit up, her damp eyes searching his in the dimness as his hand dropped to rest at her waist.

"You do?" she asked, the hope inside her swelling.

Clay's dark eyes were utterly serious. "You were just a kid," he said softly. "A kid who pulled a foolish stunt. I know you didn't mean for Angie to die."

Willa stared helplessly at him as disheartened tears swam into her eyes. He still didn't believe her, still didn't understand. Willa turned her face away and made a move to get up, but Clay didn't release her.

"I don't think Angie would be too pleased with the way things have been between you and I since then."

Willa couldn't look at Clay for a moment. When she did, she saw a tenderness and affection in his expression that surprised her.

"Angie would have wanted us to stay friends," he said. "I can see that now." Clay's fingers moved in slow circles on her back as he gripped her waist. "If there's a way for you and I to put the past five years behind us and start fresh, maybe we ought to try. What do you say?"

Willa was suddenly overcome with bittersweet emotion. Clay was forgiving her for something she hadn't done, yet offering her a reconciliation she'd not believed possible. It startled her to realize just how much she'd yearned all this time for things to come right between them, but it disappointed her that it all seemed to hinge on Clay's compassion for her rather than on the truth.

Fearful of somehow jeopardizing this truce, no matter how imperfect it was, Willa nodded slowly, bringing a trembling hand to Clay's jaw in a quick, shy caress. "All right," she murmured, the taste of new tears in her mouth as she smiled slightly and watched his eyes for any hint of insincerity.

"Good." Clay's face relaxed into a smile that eased Willa's uncertainty. "I think it would be a good idea to get our fresh start off on a full stomach. How does supper sound to you?"

Willa was too choked to answer for a moment as she sensed the first tendrils of renewed friendship forming. Surely this wasn't really happening.

"Let me have some time to freshen up and I'll see what's in the kitchen," she said as she slid off Clay's lap. Clay's hand caught hers at the last moment, enveloping her slim fingers in the hard warmth of his.

"Take your time. I'll see to supper," he said as he came to his feet.

Willa felt his fingers tighten, and she reflexively pulled back, panicked suddenly at the depth of the change that was happening between them. If Clay noticed the anxiety that made her withdraw and hurry upstairs, he didn't comment.

Willa lingered nervously in her bathroom, having splashed her face with cool water before she lightly reapplied a bit of makeup. She could hear Clay rummaging around in the kitchen and was reluctant now to join him. No one had ever seen her as he just had, not even Aunt Tess, and Willa felt uncomfortably exposed. She waited as long as she dared before she headed downstairs.

To her relief, Clay was standing at the short length of counter beside the stove with his back to her as she entered the kitchen.

"Still like your eggs over easy?" he asked as he heard her walk in.

"Over easy is fine," she answered cautiously, suddenly suspicious of Clay's earlier behavior. Perhaps he'd just felt sorry for her. Some men seemed to have trouble dealing with women's tears, and though it shamed Willa to acknowledge it, she'd just put on one heck of a show. Was it too farfetched to wonder if Clay's gentleness with her—and his willingness to forgive her—was motivated more by pity and male embarrassment than by genuine feelings? She had to find out.

Uneasy, and uncertain about just how she could discern something like that, Willa crossed to where Clay stood laying strips of bacon in a large iron skillet.

"Is there anything I can do?" she offered, watching his profile intently until his dark eyes swung toward hers.

"You could set the table."

Willa turned away to do so, noticing as she got out plates and silverware that a chocolate aroma was beginning to fill the kitchen, mingling deliciously with the smell of frying bacon.

"You don't mind bacon and eggs for a late supper, do you?" Clay asked as he watched her set the table while he waited for the bacon to cook.

"As long as it's someone else's cooking, I could eat just about anything that isn't a TV dinner," she replied.

One corner of Clay's mouth lifted. "I take it you don't like to cook."

"I don't get a lot of practice," she said without thinking. Alarmed at the bit of information she'd just given away, Willa glanced down and gave more attention than necessary to laying the flatware just right. Most larger ranches had a cook to prepare meals for the ranch hands. Clay would never guess that the cook on the D & R worked for Willa.

"I never did hear where it is you've been working the past few years," Clay said.

Willa was instantly alert. She didn't want anyone here poking into the life she'd made for herself in Colorado. Her life there was productive and secure. She was well thought of and there was no way she'd even flirt with the possibility of jeopardizing that. "I've worked several places," she answered noncommittally. "Mostly Kansas, Colorado...." She shrugged as she let her voice trail off.

"Paige said you've worked with horses," Clay persisted.

Willa turned away and opened the refrigerator door to get out a carton of milk. "I prefer working with horses," she told him evasively before smoothly changing the subject. "There's some orange juice concentrate in the freezer. Want me to make it up?"

Clay didn't ask her any more questions, but as they finished getting their meal together, Willa caught his speculative gaze on her several times and sensed his curiosity. She forgot all about it, however, when they sat down to bacon, eggs and toast, and the oven buzzer sounded.

"I saw the mix for this in the cupboard and thought it sounded good." Clay gingerly removed a pan of brownies from the oven, with the help of a tiny crocheted potholder meant more for decoration than practical use. He shifted the pan first one way then another to keep from getting his fingers scorched through the open crochet pattern. The brownies finally made it to the table with a thud and a muted curse.

"They look wonderful," Willa commented, doing her best to suppress a smile as Clay flung the potholder down and settled on his chair.

Clay caught the emerald sparkle in Willa's eyes and did a double take. It had been a long time since he'd seen anything in her even remotely resembling the impish, carefree adolescent she had been—the one he'd been so powerfully attracted to—and he suddenly ached to see her that way again.

Willa watched the darkening of Clay's eyes with more than a little apprehension. He was staring at her so intently that she felt as if the midnight black of his gaze would swallow her whole. Something contracted deep down inside her as a primitive element of her psyche understood the look and began to respond. Alarmed at the erratic skittering of her pulse, Willa fled the contact with Clay. She hastily lifted a fork of fried egg to her mouth and tried to chew normally, unnerved beyond belief.

"I've made arrangements to have the horses you planned to sell picked up and taken to the stock auction at the Cascade fairgrounds tomorrow," Clay said to break the uncomfortable silence between them as they finished their meal.

Willa glanced up, the flash of irritation she felt melding into a feeling of inevitability. No matter what she thought seemed to be changing between them, Clay was still determined to hurry her departure. Suddenly she didn't feel like resisting him. "Sounds good," she answered as she pushed her plate slightly away from herself and leaned back in her chair a moment. Her wrist was aching and she flexed her fingers beneath the table, hoping to ease the pain.

"You don't think I was out of line making those arrangements?" he asked, his gaze sharpening as he studied the faint lines of strain on her face.

Willa managed a thin smile. "Do you want an argument?"

"I might."

Willa pushed back her chair and stood to clear the table. "If you make any more arrangements for the Circle H without consulting me first, you'll probably get one." She finished stacking the plates as Clay rose to help her.

"I'll get those," he said, taking the small stack from her and carrying it to the sink.

Willa got out the dish soap and started running the dishwater, but Clay nudged her aside, handing her a dish towel.

"You don't want to get that bandage wet," he pointed out, and Willa watched with some amusement as Clay awkwardly set about washing the dishes, cringing when he banged a glass against the faucet and nearly dropped one of her aunt's good plates. But in no time, the dishes were done and put away.

"You're fairly competent in the kitchen," Willa remarked as Clay finished wiping off the stove and hanging up the dishcloth.

"I've had to cook for myself once or twice," he answered as he unrolled his shirt sleeves and rebuttoned them. He nodded toward her wrist. "I'd like to have a look at that before I go."

Willa shrugged, unconcerned. "It's still a little sore, but it's fine."

Clay reached for her left hand and gently pushed her sleeve up well past the bandage. Willa was stunned by the myriad sensations Clay's touch set off as he tenderly inspected the area around the bandage. Though her wrist still ached, there was no sign of further swelling or discoloration around or above the bandage, which the doctor had cautioned her to watch for.

"Will you be all right alone tonight?" Clay asked as he tugged down her sleeve but continued to hold her hand.

Willa looked up, her senses careening at Clay's nearness as the sensual attraction she'd been fighting to suppress came charging through her system. The combined scent of after-shave and leather invaded her nostrils and Willa felt more than a little overwhelmed.

"I don't know why not," she answered, dismayed at the breathless quality in her voice. "Thanks for...everything," she added, managing to pull her hand from Clay's grasp.

The moment they touched a current of excitement passed wildly between them. As if unable to resist the frisson, Clay reached for her.

Slowly, as though the moment were frail, he pulled her against him. Willa stared at his shirt front, frightened at what she sensed was coming. Contact with the male heat of Clay's body sent a tingling weakness through her and her eyes drifted closed as he placed a lean, calloused finger beneath her chin and lifted her face.

"We can't," she pleaded softly as she felt Clay's lips brush hers in a feather-light caress.

"Some things are inevitable, Willa," he whispered as his mouth continued to move enticingly across hers. "You can fight them only so long."

Willa's hands slipped around Clay's middle and locked behind his back as his arms tightened on her waist like steel bands. With each caressing stroke of his mouth, something wild was being ignited inside her, something that demanded fulfillment no matter what the cost.

Suddenly terrified, Willa managed to evade his lips, and pressed her flushed cheek against his neck. "We have to stop," she whispered, shivering with pure pleasure as his tongue found her ear and began toying with the lobe. "Please, Clay."

"All right," he relented as he gradually loosened his hold. "Maybe we are rushing things." Clay's hands lingered at her waist.

Willa shook her head. "This shouldn't be happening between us at all, Clay. It can't." *Besides, there's no real trust between us. And there never can be as long as you believe Paige,* her heart added silently.

Willa pushed away and stepped back. "It's getting late." She couldn't look at him, but felt his eyes on her as he reached for his Stetson.

"You know the phone number at Orion. I expect you to use it if you need anything tonight," he said as he put on his hat and tugged the brim into place.

Willa glanced up, then away. "I'll be fine."

"I'll be over for the horses before ten tomorrow. My men are taking care of most everything else, so you might as well sleep in." Clay hesitated long enough for Willa to look up at him again. "Good night."

Willa's voice went husky with the mad swirl of emotions that suddenly engulfed her. "Good night, Clay."

WILLA WORKED SILENTLY at grooming the aging bay, the last of the four horses she'd decided should go to the sale in town. She'd been at this for the past two hours, trimming manes, cutting burrs from tails, and now she was carefully hosing down the big animal before she gave it a final brushing, hoping the extra care she took with grooming would ensure a better price for each animal at the auction.

All four horses—two sorrels, a buckskin and the bay—were past their prime and, Willa judged, at just about the age when they would begin to cost the ranch in vet bills. Even taking into account that they hadn't been receiving the kind of workouts they needed to keep them in condition, none of the horses would have been her choice for working cattle. She'd taken time to try out each mount in the weeks she'd been there and had concluded that although the bay and sorrel geldings were gentle and well mannered enough for children, neither quite had the stamina or savvy to work cattle. The other sorrel had particularly bad habits that made her hard to handle and the buckskin mare's penchant for being easily spooked had already landed Willa in the dust more than once. The men she eventually hired would need sturdy, much more reliable mounts than these to work the almost wild cattle on the Circle H.

Willa had just finished grooming the bay and tying it with the others, when Clay pulled in with a four-horse goose-neck stock trailer behind his pickup. She gathered up the grooming brushes, combs and clothes as he drove the pickup in a wide circle in the barnyard so the truck was headed back toward the drive before he switched off the engine.

Tamping down the sudden shyness she felt as the events of the night before flashed through her mind, Willa tossed everything into the wooden box just inside the tack room and walked to the front of the barn.

"You're looking a little pale," Clay remarked as he approached, his dark eyes going over her, taking particular note of the damp muddy spatters on her jeans. "I thought the doctor told you to take it easy for the next few days."

"He did," she returned. Then, determined to rebuff his concern, she gestured toward the horses tethered along the stable aisle. "The horses are ready if you are." At Clay's nod, Willa turned and walked into the barn to untie the bay and one of the sorrels, while Clay opened the back gate of the trailer.

Both horses loaded easily, as did the second sorrel, but the moment Willa led the skittish buckskin to the trailer, the animal drew back on the lead rope and shied nervously.

"Let me get this one, Willa," Clay said as he took a step toward her.

"No, she's fine." Willa moved to block Clay, taking hold of the lead rope with both hands as she did so. Speaking softly to calm the wary animal, Willa led her forward again. The mare shied slightly a second time, but allowed Willa to guide her.

All went well until the mare's hooves hit the metal floor of the trailer. Suddenly the big animal threw her head, then reared back, half dragging Willa with her. The swift jerk on the lead rope sent shafts of pain through Willa's arm as she fought to cling to the rope and regain her balance. Clay was at her side instantly, cursing through gritted teeth as he grabbed the rope and looped it around the mare's nose to choke her down as she bolted sideways and pulled him halfway across the wide drive. Unable to help, Willa got out of the way to give Clay room to maneuver.

Once the mare realized that fighting Clay caused the noose around her nose to tighten and close off her supply of air, she slowly calmed and submitted to Clay's control. In moments Clay had her loaded. While he secured the animals and closed the tailgate, Willa leaned against the side of the trailer, waiting for the throbbing pain in her injured wrist to ease.

"Damn it, Willa." Clay's face was stony with anger as he came around the back of the trailer.

Willa straightened self-consciously and stopped cradling her arm, automatically wanting to conceal her discomfort from Clay.

"Where does your kind of stubbornness come from, anyway?" he ranted.

"Probably from the same place yours does," she shot back as she headed for the house. "I'll meet you at the fairgrounds with the papers just as soon as I get cleaned up and get my clothes changed."

"I'll wait."

Willa hesitated at the words, then stopped and turned back toward Clay. "I intend to go to that auction," she told him coldly, not about to turn the papers over to him and sit at home. Besides, the bids were higher if someone rode each horse around the ring while the bidding was going on. She had to try to get the best possible price for the horses, since the cost of replacing them was going to be hard given her aunt's depleted resources.

"No one said you couldn't," Clay said, his stony expression unchanging. "There any reason why you can't ride to town with me?"

Willa stifled her surprise. "I can think of a few reasons," she said quietly.

"Like what?"

"You know what." Willa's voice had gone softer. "And I should stop over and have this bandage seen to at some point." Her breath caught at the way Clay's dark eyes suddenly dropped to her arm, then veered to made a slow sweep of her body. The heat that flashed over her skin when his gaze lingered too long had nothing to do with standing in the warm morning sunshine. Willa was vividly reminded of what it had felt like to be in his arms with his lips playing sensually with hers.

"I've got nothing but time today, Willa," he said, his deep voice low and faintly rough as his eyes came up to meet hers. Willa couldn't move for a moment as their gazes clung.

"You're sure?"

"More sure than I've been about anything for a long time," he answered gravely, and Willa felt a wild clash of dread and excitement.

"I won't be long," she said as she turned and walked quickly toward the house.

Scarcely ten minutes later, she emerged from the house in new jeans and a long-sleeved gold plaid shirt that intensified the green in her eyes and highlighted the sunny glints in the sandy brown hair that fell past her shoulders from beneath her Stetson. Avoiding Clay's eyes as he leaned against the truck bed on the passenger side of the pickup and watched her, Willa tossed her purse through the open window of the cab and was about to head to the Circle H pickup for the saddles she'd loaded in the back earlier, when Clay's voice stopped her.

"Already got the saddles," he said as he straightened and levered open the passenger door for her. Willa hesitated, then brushed past him to climb in, feeling an odd spurt of relief when he closed the door and moved away from her to walk around the front of the truck to the driver's side. That relief evaporated the moment he slid behind the wheel and reached for the key in the ignition.

"You're strung up tight as a fiddle, Willa. Relax," he advised as he gave the key a twist and the big engine rumbled to life. "Let's just let things happen naturally between us."

Surprised at his candor, Willa glanced sideways and released a pent-up breath of nervousness and exasperation. "I can't believe this is what you really want, Clay." Willa watched his profile carefully and decided to speak her mind. "I don't want your friendship because you were swayed by a few tears last night."

"That's good, honey," he said, turning to fix his dark eyes on her face, "because I'm not sure that what's going to happen between you and me has a whole lot to do with ordinary friendship."

Willa was speechless for a moment. "Maybe I don't want anything more than friendship," she said stiffly as she forced herself to maintain eye contact with him and conceal the truth.

Clay watched her steadily. "Am I reading the signals wrong, green eyes?"

Caught off guard by the old pet name, Willa couldn't answer. The denial lodged in her throat.

"I didn't think so," he said softly, then turned his head to check the mirrors before he put the truck into gear.

CHAPTER EIGHT

EVERYTHING'S HAPPENING TOO QUICKLY, Willa thought as she looked down from her seat in the stands and watched Clay ride the jittery buckskin into the sale ring as the auctioneer opened the bidding.

The attraction that had hovered between them since their reconciliation the night before was beginning to escalate, overwhelming her emotions and her good sense. She knew this renewed relationship was still too fragile for her to allow it to get confused with something as intense and distracting as physical desire—it was too soon for that.

Yet Willa couldn't take her eyes from the man in the ring. Her attention was riveted to his every move; she was unable to focus clearly on anything else. Clay rode the fractious buckskin with the skill of a man who'd been a good rider from early childhood, a man so thoroughly in control that the horse instinctively obeyed him. Few animals would argue with a rider Clay's size, and yet he didn't manhandle the buckskin.

Willa's eyes dropped to the large work-calloused hands that held the reins and she was instantly reminded of what they'd felt like the night before, when he'd held her and soothed away her tears. Dismayed at the strange fluttering in the pit of her stomach, Willa lifted her gaze, only to find it straying once more to his wide shoulders, his spare middle and his hard-muscled thighs.

Embarrassment brought her eyes determinedly upward as Clay rode the buckskin around the ring one more time before he dismounted and pulled the saddle to give the bidders a better look at the mare.

To distract herself, she glanced into the stands of wooden bleachers that surrounded the ring. Willa recognized the majority of bidders and spectators to be locals, then frowned when she spotted a handful who were not—and who might be bidding for a meat packer. That meant there was a possibility that the Circle H horses could end up as dog food. Willa reached up and adjusted her hat brim uncomfortably as she turned her attention back toward the ring. When the bidding stopped, Clay released the buckskin to a ringman to be led from the ring and set aside in a pen for the buyer.

Once by one, Clay rode each of the other three horses into the ring. Though all four sold for less than she'd hoped, Willa felt a bit better that each one had gone to a different bidder—all locals.

"I thought we agreed I'd do all the work," Clay reminded her later when she joined him at the holding pens to help carry the saddles back to the trailer.

"It doesn't look like you left any," she remarked as he hefted one of the last two saddles to his shoulder and let the other dangle from his fingers at his side. Willa gathered up the bridles he'd draped over the fence and followed him to the trailer.

"Didn't you see anything you'd like to bid on?" he asked as he stowed the saddles in the trailer and turned to reach for the bridles she was holding.

"Nothing special," she said with a shrug. "I think I'd rather shop around a little and buy something privately." There was too much room for error in buying a horse at an auction and Willa wasn't about to gamble with her aunt's dwindling resources.

"I've got a couple of four-year-olds I might consider selling," Clay told her as he finished with the tack and stepped down to close the trailer. "Nothing too fancy, but they're sound and they've been worked some. I can show them to you later on today if you're up to it."

"Sounds good," Willa said, forcing a smile to her lips. It was hot standing in the sun and the dust. She wasn't used to feeling tired in the middle of the day and the aspirin she'd taken that morning to blunt the dull pain in her wrist had worn off a long time ago.

"I hope you made arrangements for the bookkeeper to mail you the check for the sale of your horses," Clay said pointedly as he surveyed the increasing pallor of Willa's cheeks.

Willa stiffened, automatically trying to stand a little straighter and not look as wilted as she felt. "Of course I did. That's the way it's done here, isn't it?" Without waiting for him to answer, she started around the trailer to the passenger side of the truck and got in, releasing a tired sigh as she tugged off her hat and leaned her head back.

She listened to the reassuring sound of Clay checking the trailer, then reluctantly lifted her head and replaced her hat when she heard him make his way around to the driver's side.

"Are you ready to get that dressing changed?" he asked as he opened the door and climbed in, his dark eyes flicking down to her bandaged wrist, which rested on her thigh.

"I think I'd rather have some lunch first," she answered, then added, "and since you refused to let me pay you the going rate for trailering and showing the horses, it'll be my treat."

"Your treat, huh?" Clay repeated with a grin as he slid the key into the ignition and started the truck. "How about that little steak house over on the highway?"

WILLA STOOD next to Clay in the elevator, relieved that they were finished at the hospital and would at last be going home. After having her dressing seen to and changed, they had stopped to visit Aunt Tess. One look at the deep lines of worry and concern on her aunt's face told Willa Tess had found out about the snakebite, and Willa had spent the entire visit trying to allay Tess's fears.

"Thanks for helping me with Aunt Tess," Willa murmured, then turned her head to look up at Clay as the elevator slowed to a stop and the doors swished open. "She listens to you."

"It's not that she doesn't listen to you, Willa," Clay said as he placed his hand at the back of her waist and escorted her forward. "She was worried. She's laid up and couldn't be there to help you. Plus she probably figures she was the one who put you in harm's way in the first place."

"I can't stand the thought of her worrying," Willa said on a quaver of emotion. "She shouldn't be upset in any way."

Clay's hand slid around her waist and brought her against his side as they walked down the corridor toward the exit that led to the parking lot. Willa's arm instinctively found its way around Clay's lean middle in response.

"Tess is getting stronger every day. Besides, she's going to have to learn to deal with upsets without letting them affect her health."

"But this is too soon for her," Willa insisted, her mind filled with the memory of her aunt's collapse and her part in causing it, not to mention that Tess was still grieving for Cal.

"It's been almost four weeks, Willa," he reminded her, his arm tightening on her waist reassuringly. "She's going to be released from the hospital within the next two or three days."

"But you saw how tired she looked—and the way her hands were shaking...." Willa's voice caught on the words as her throat knotted with emotion.

"I saw," Clay agreed as they passed through the automatic doors to the parking lot and started toward the far end, where he'd left the truck and trailer. "She looked just the way you do now—tired, worked up... and about to cry."

Startled at the observation, Willa pursed her lips as she struggled to bring her emotions under control. She still felt deeply embarrassed about her crying jag the night before, and she wasn't about to treat Clay to another one.

The ride out of town passed in companionable silence. Neither spoke until they approached the turnoff to Orion.

"You still up to looking at those horses?"

"Might as well," she answered as she shifted into a slightly more erect position. The ride from town had made her drowsy and she felt impatient with herself for her lack of stamina.

"We can always do this tomorrow," he reminded her, but Willa shook her head.

"Unless it's more convenient for you to wait until tomorrow, I'd just as soon take care of this now."

Clay signaled, then turned into the graveled drive that stretched more than a mile to the Orion ranch house. Once they passed the house and took the right fork to the barns and the network of corrals beyond, Clay angled the truck and trailer to the side of the lane and switched off the engine.

In only a few minutes one of Clay's men had brought up the two horses and put them into a corral. After Willa had looked over both sorrels, Clay had them saddled and taken to a small pasture where a half-dozen cows and their calves waited.

Standing next to Clay, Willa rested her forearms on a chest-high rail of board fencing, cushioning her injured wrist on top of her other one as she looked through the rails. She watched thoughtfully as two of Clay's men worked the bunch, gathering, roping, then separating out a calf or two to show each horse's abilities.

"I thought you said they were nothing fancy," Willa said, never taking her eyes from the horses, clearly satisfied with both animals.

"I meant that they don't have the flash and the polish of the kind of horses you're used to."

Willa felt a tremor of alarm go through her at his words. She turned her head and glanced at Clay, catching the glimmer of interest in his dark eyes. "What makes you think that?" she asked as casually as she could manage.

"Tess said you worked for a big horse breeder in Colorado." The speculation in Clay's eyes deepened and Willa felt herself close up inside.

"Not so big," she said dismissively, and looked back toward the horses. "What kind of price are you looking to get?"

Clay didn't answer right away. Willa felt him study her profile for a few moments before he seemed to accept her evasive response. He named a price that made her frown.

"That's way too low, Clay. I can't let you just give them to me."

"I won't be 'giving' them to you. I'll be 'giving' them to the Hardings."

Willa chafed at the not-so-subtle reminder that Clay was only doing business through her, not with her.

"I've already agreed to let you do more than Aunt Tess would be comfortable with. I can't let you do this, too." Willa quickly named a price she felt was fairer.

Clay released an impatient sigh, then reached up to readjust his hat before he tugged it down to a determined angle over his eyes. "This is no time to be stubborn, Willa."

"I'm not being stubborn," she countered as she dropped her arms from the fence and turned to face him. "I'm offering you a fair price."

"I'm not asking for one."

"Why not?" she demanded.

Clay's expression was a mixture of irritation and discomfort. "Things turned out to be a lot worse at the Circle H than I thought they were. If I had known how much worse, I would have found a way to get around Tess's pride and done something about it a long time ago."

"You can't help someone who won't let you," Willa reminded him.

"No kidding," he muttered as he stared down at her meaningfully. Willa had to restrain a smile.

"What about the horses?" he pressed, his no-nonsense tone of voice softened by the sparkle of affection in his dark eyes.

Taken aback by the warm look, Willa glanced away, an odd kind of pain in her chest as the deep feelings she had for him came bursting up. He'd been generous enough already, sending men to work for her who were still on his payroll—men he needed to work on Orion—not to mention what he'd done to help her today, plus his agreement to help her find someone to work the Circle II full-time. She couldn't let him do all that, then allow him to sell good horses to her at half their market value.

Willa took a deep breath and shook her head, her eyes coming back to meet Clay's. "I can't pay you any less than my offer. If you won't take it, then I guess we won't be doing business today."

Clay didn't reply. His expression hardened and the soft light went out of his eyes as he glanced over her head toward where his men waited with the horses.

Willa watched the mild flash of anger come over Clay and was suddenly conscious of how precarious their renewed friendship was. The reconciliation that was barely twenty-four hours old was still far too easily imperiled and Willa felt a spurt of panic as she acknowledged how quickly a wrong word or misinterpreted action might divide them.

And in her mind it followed that if Clay were ever in the position of doubting her again, his lack of trust could end their friendship—permanently, this time.

"Miss Ross will be buying both horses, Ed," he called out. "Go ahead and load them in the trailer and take them to the Circle H."

"If you don't mind, I'd like to ride over with your men," Willa told him, the pleasure of finding two very satisfactory horses dampened. "I'll send your check back with them later."

Clay's gaze swung back to hers, but the hardness still lingered in his expression. "I was hoping you'd stay to supper."

Willa shook her head, suddenly determined to flee the ill-fated attraction she felt for him. "It's been a long day, Clay. I'd just like to go home."

"Then I'll take you in the car. Give me a minute," he said as he turned away and met his men at the pasture gate.

Relieved to be going home even if it was Clay who was taking her there, Willa started walking toward the house, where his car was parked, stopping by the truck to retrieve her purse. After a quick trip into the house for the paperwork on the horses, Clay joined her and they started for the Circle H.

"The boys'll be taking care of the chores tonight when they bring the horses over," Clay said when they reached the Circle H ranch house and he switched off the engine.

Willa tossed him an impatient look as she levered her door open. "You're doing too much, Clay," she said, stepping out when he did, her gaze meeting his over the roof of the car.

"We had an agreement, didn't we?"

Willa closed her door with a snap, reminded not only of the agreement, but of the motivation behind it: to force her to leave Cascade as soon as possible.

The faint signs of strain and tiredness on her face deepened fractionally as she nodded. "I'll get your check."

Clay followed her into the house, handing her the papers for the horses as she seated herself at the desk in the den to write out the check. She had just finished signing her name, when the telephone shrilled. She reached for the receiver.

"Circle H."

The room went quiet for only a moment. "Deke? How're things going?" she asked as she smiled, the call obviously welcome.

Clay watched the weariness disappear from Willa's face. She was smiling, even chuckling, at something this caller was saying. The warm affection in her voice was something he hadn't heard in years.

"Is the boss-lady back from St. Louis?" she asked making a veiled reference to her partner, Ivy, as she rolled the pen between her thumb and forefinger and listened. "She did? Good. I was hoping she'd go out to have a look at that one." Another pause. "I don't know yet. She'll be out of the hospital soon, but I haven't hired anyone."

The room went still enough for Clay to faintly hear the deep masculine voice coming across the line.

"You miss me, huh?" Willa asked as she leaned back in the swivel chair for a few moments. "No, don't send anyone up. It would complicate things here. I'll find someone locally." Willa glanced toward Clay. "Aunt Tess's neighbor has a lead on a foreman, and once he's hired, someone will turn up."

Willa's eyes slid from Clay's as she gave her attention to something else Deke was asking. "It's a long story, Deke," she said, the weariness creeping back into her expression as Deke made a remark. "Yeah," she answered, smiling wryly, "one of those. Anything else?" Willa listened for a moment, then ended the conversation and leaned over to hang up the phone. Clay's eyes were fixed on her with telling intensity.

"This Deke sounds a little eager for you to get back to Colorado."

The harsh edge in Clay's voice threw her for a moment.

"He's the foreman of the ranch where I work," she answered truthfully, then looked down and folded the check along the perforations.

"Is that all he is to you?"

Willa tore the check out of the ledger-sized pad, surprised at Clay's directness. "He's also a very good friend," she added as she looked up and passed him the check.

Clay took the slip of paper but barely glanced at it. "Which ranch is it you work on down there?"

Willa closed the check pad and stood to lock it in one of the metal cabinets behind the desk. She didn't answer until her back was toward him. "Just a small one. You've probably never heard of it." She was attempting to sound casual, but she was a jumble of nerves. Clay wasn't about to let her evade the question and they both knew it.

"Try me."

"I'd rather not," she said firmly as she closed the cabinet before she turned to pick up the papers and skim them before she consigned them to a file.

"Why not?"

Willa exhaled a pent-up breath, then jammed the papers into the file and shoved the drawer closed. Other than telling an outright lie, the only alternative to evasion was to tell Clay to mind his own business. And telling him that would be tantamount to waving a red flag in front of a bull.

"You're supposed to take the hint and back off," she said candidly as she turned and met the mistrust in his eyes. Stung by the look, Willa's gaze ricocheted away. "Your men should be here anytime now," she said as she headed around the desk. "I need to go out and—"

Clay caught her arm gently as she stepped past him.

"You haven't even told Tess, have you?" he concluded gruffly, his disapproval evident. "What little she knows, she's had to guess. Isn't that right?" Willa made a slight move to test the firmness of his grip. Clay lowered his voice. "Why, Willa? Why don't you trust either of us enough to answer such a simple question?"

"Why don't you trust me enough to leave it alone?" she shot back, resenting the guilt Clay made her feel.

"I thought things had changed between us."

"Not everything," she burst out, then instantly regretted the words. She tried to pull away, but Clay caught her other arm and turned her fully toward him.

"Care to explain that?"

"No, I don't," she told him coolly, forcing herself to look up into his stern countenance. "Now if you don't mind..."

"I *do* mind," Clay growled as his thumbs began to rub in calming circles on her arms. Willa's gaze fled his. She was panicked by the sensuality that radiated over her at the small gentle movements. "But it doesn't look like it'll do me any good," he added as he allowed her to pull away and take a step back. Willa felt chilled by the abrupt release. Warily her gaze came back to meet the frustration in Clay's.

It distressed her that she couldn't seem to reveal to him something as small as the details of her life in Colorado. Besides, if Paige found out about the D & R through something Clay might say, Willa was certain her cousin would find a way to use the information against her. And Willa couldn't bring herself to take the risk until she felt more secure about the reconciliation with Clay. There was also her partner to consider.

"How soon can you get that man from Sheridan down here for an interview?" she asked briskly. "You said his sister lives in Laramie. Is it possible to get him here within the next few days?"

"I can ask," Clay replied, his grim expression hardening as he accepted the swift change of subject. "I'll give him a call tonight."

Willa nodded her satisfaction. "Good. Please do that. Let me know how soon I can see him. If he seems a good choice at all, I'll hire him."

"Just like that?" Clay's voice was harsh.

"Why not?" she challenged, meeting the hard look in his eyes without flinching. "I promised I wouldn't make excuses to keep things going."

One corner of Clay's mouth hitched up in an unamused line. "No one said you had to hire the first man who comes along, either."

"I'll hire the best person available for the job," she told him curtly, "whether it's the man from Sheridan or someone else."

Clay studied the obstinate set of her features for a few moments before his expression softened. "I don't want to fight, Willa."

The quiet words cooled the anger she felt. "Neither do I," she admitted on a wavering breath.

"And I'm not exactly sure I want you to hurry back to Colorado."

Willa was stunned at the impact those few words had on her emotions and she felt herself scrambling to negate the instant meaning her heart assigned them. Clay moved forward into the short space between them, hesitating fractionally as his hands came up to rest on her waist.

"And I wasn't prying into your life down there in order to make trouble. It's just that there are a lot of things I don't know about you that I want to."

Slowly, as if giving her those scant moments to adjust, Clay lowered his head and touched his lips to hers. The tiny explosion of desire that burst deep inside her at the tender force of his mouth spread through every part of her until her entire being ached with longing. And when Clay suddenly crushed her to him, Willa's arms came up and locked around his neck. The fierceness of their feelings left them both bruised and breathless when Clay finally dragged his lips from hers.

"I've wanted to do that all day," he rasped as he appeared to struggle for self-control. Willa's unwilling sound of agreement brought his mouth back to hers with a pleasured groan. Neither of them heard the slam of the porch door or the rapid clatter of heels across the kitchen, quickly muffled by the carpet in the hall.

Paige's belatedly called "Anybody home?" caught them both by surprise as she burst through the open door to the den.

Startled, Willa drew back and broke off the kiss, but Clay didn't release her.

Near the doorway, Paige stood frozen almost in midstep at the sight of them in each other's arms. Alarm and uncertainty showed plainly on her lovely features before she seemed to recover herself.

"Well, well." Paige's voice was a bit more shrill than normal as her turbulent gaze flicked from one to the other. "It looks as if the black sheep has managed to work her way back into the fold, after all."

CHAPTER NINE

WITH OBVIOUS RELUCTANCE Clay loosened his hold and allowed Willa to take a half step away, his eyes searching hers as Paige's implication hit home.

"Willa and I have resolved our differences, if that's what you mean," he said as he turned to Paige, his unsmiling expression effectively communicating his displeasure with her remark.

Quickly taking her cue, Paige was contrite. "I suppose my comment was a bit uncalled for," she admitted with a brittle smile. Willa was surprised Paige didn't choke on the words. "It's just such a shock to see the two of you...together like that. After all..." Paige let the words drift off, knowing full well she didn't have to say more to remind either one of them of the reason for their differences.

The sound of a pickup truck and horse trailer rolling past the house to the barn out back was a welcome intrusion. Clay's men had arrived.

"I've got some horses to get settled in," Willa said, grateful for the excuse to escape the chaotic mixture of fear and suppressed rage that seemed to emanate in invisible waves from her cousin. Though Willa intended to leave Clay and Paige alone together, she was pleased when Clay followed her outside and fell into step beside her.

"I thought you might want some time alone with Paige," Willa said, suddenly needing to press Clay into a declaration of some sort.

"Why is that?"

Willa shrugged. "She's been gone a few days..." She didn't finish the sentence.

"So you think I might want to smooth things over and make up for lost time?" he said, the gruffness in his voice a mild rebuke. "I don't think you've been paying attention to what's been going on between you and me, Willa."

Clay caught her arm and gently swung her around to face him. Willa glanced self-consciously at the Orion ranch hands who were opening the trailer and about to unload the horses, but the angle of the parked vehicle prevented the couple from being seen. Clay's gaze followed the direction of hers before he backed her against the thick trunk of one of the oak trees in the backyard and bent his head to kiss her soundly.

"Now that we've straightened that out," he growled when he finally released her and left her limp against the rough bark at her back, "I think we'd better get down to the barn and see to those horses."

Willa opened passion-glazed eyes to the self-assured, supremely male look Clay was giving her, her emotions still reeling. The corners of her mouth curved up softly as she reached for the hand he held out to her, her cousin forgotten as she allowed him to tug her away from the tree trunk and slip his arm around her waist for the walk to the barn.

"HAVE YOU FORGOTTEN our little talk, or do you just no longer care about Mother's health?"

Now that Clay had gone home, Paige didn't hesitate to launch her attack. Once she'd surmised that whatever was going on between Willa and Clay hadn't exposed her yet, she was more determined than ever to ensure Willa's silence.

Willa looked up from prying off her boots and setting them in their usual place on the back porch, annoyed that she'd barely got in the door before Paige had started her harangue. "Can't this wait until tomorrow?" she asked, stepping past her cousin with the intention of heading upstairs to her room for the night.

Paige turned to follow her. "No, it can't," she said firmly, catching up with Willa in the hall. "Just how far have things gone between you and Clay?" she demanded, putting out a professionally manicured hand to grab Willa's arm and stop her.

Willa gasped at the pain as Paige clutched at her and unintentionally caught her injured wrist. Paige hesitated for a moment, surprised to feel the squared padding beneath Willa's sleeve, then quickly released her.

"What's the matter with you? Are you hurt?" Paige asked, the belligerence in her voice subdued somewhat by the obvious flash of pain on Willa's face.

Willa's lips formed a thin line. "Nothing for you to trouble yourself about," she said, then took the opportunity to turn and start up the stairway as the pain slowly subsided.

"What do you mean by that?" Paige's steps echoed Willa's all the way to the top.

"Don't you have other things besides my health to worry about?" Willa asked, unable to resist needling her cousin. As she'd expected, Paige had easily forgotten her small show of concern.

"I asked you how far things had gone between you and Clay," Paige repeated as she followed Willa into her room. "And while you're at it, how did you manage to get on his good side in the first place? What did you tell him?" Paige's violet eyes were a bit wild now.

Willa looked away and exhaled a tired breath as she tugged her shirttail from the waist of her jeans and walked toward her bathroom. Paige followed her right to the door and used her hand to prevent Willa from closing it all the way.

"I haven't told Clay any of your secrets," Willa answered wearily as she finished unbuttoning her blouse, then leaned over the tub to turn on the faucets.

Paige's voice sounded a little less anxious after that. "Then what about you and Clay?" she persisted over the sound of running water. "What's going on between the two of you?"

Willa didn't answer for a moment. She'd wondered about that, too. "Just a little mutual attraction," she called back, knowing her answer sounded annoyingly vague.

"Then you won't mind breaking it off with him," Paige said, her imperious tone of voice telling Willa plainly that she fully expected her to do just that.

Willa felt herself slump a bit at the order, saddened that she and her own flesh-and-blood relative were so deeply at odds. "Sorry," she called out, knowing full well she was tossing down the gauntlet to the one person in her life more than capable of taking it up.

THE NEXT TWO DAYS were predictably difficult as Willa tried to adjust to both Paige's presence in the house and the preparations for her aunt's release from the hospital.

Aunt Tess's earlier plans to stay with Mabel Asner in town had changed and she would be returning to the Circle H directly. Willa guessed Tess had wearied of her overbearing friend's frequent visits to the hospital and had developed second thoughts about staying with her. The fact that Paige was planning to be home for at least the next several days had probably given Tess a polite excuse to turn down Mabel's hospitality.

Not one to be easily thwarted, Mabel accompanied Tess home, anyway, her determination to see her settled in putting a damper on the cheerful event for Willa.

"Willa ought to be able to take care of the heavy housework and cooking," Mabel was saying to Tess as Willa carried a couple of the plants her aunt had received in the hospital into the living room, where the two women were sitting with Paige. Paige cast Willa a catty look and Mabel babbled on as if Willa weren't there. "She's supposed to be hiring men to work outside. No reason for her to leave all the inside work to Paige."

Willa gritted her teeth at Mabel's critical, ill-informed comment as she set the plants down carefully on an end table.

"Willa's doing so much for me now, Mabel," Tess spoke up, firmly correcting the woman. "I don't know how I could ask her for another thing."

Willa returned the fond smile Tess sent her way, then started back out to her car for another armload of her aunt's things. To her relief, Mabel was just getting up to leave as she came back in.

"You'll have to stop all this running in and out with those things for a while. Your aunt needs a nap," Mabel told her, the stern, disapproving look on the woman's puffy face making her look more shrewish than ever as she gave pointed attention to the chambray work shirt and faded jeans Willa had worn to the hospital. Paige had dressed in a smart linen suit, but Willa hadn't bothered to change from the clothes she'd worn earlier that morning to check on the cattle. Since she knew she'd be the one taking care of Tess's belongings, Willa had seen no point in dressing up.

"Stop nagging the girl, Mabel." This time Tess was clearly irritated. "What little noise she makes would never disturb me."

"Thank you for your concern, Mrs. Asner," Willa said, straining to be pleasant and hurry the woman along at the same time. "We'll take good care of Aunt Tess. She'll do just fine."

Mabel nodded, but her look of disapproval didn't alter until she glanced over at Paige. "Come along with me a moment, would you, dear? I'd like to talk to you a bit before I leave," she said, her intent for privacy clear as she bustled past Willa to the front door.

I'll just bet, Willa thought unkindly as Paige rose gracefully to follow the short, thick-waisted matron to her car.

"Lord in heaven that woman's a busybody!" Tess exclaimed the moment the door closed and Mabel stepped out of earshot. "I don't know how I could have ever entertained the idea of staying with her in town. I would have gone crazy for sure."

Willa burst out laughing at Tess's vehemence.

"And I'm sorry she was so rude to you. I'll have a talk with her about that later." Tess braced a thin hand on the arm of the sofa and got carefully to her feet. Willa automatically reached over to assist her, but Tess waved her away. "Now don't you fuss, young lady." Tess's gray eyes came up to meet Willa's, though she had to tip her head back a bit to compensate for her smaller stature. "Just give me a hug."

Willa stepped close and hugged her aunt, the taste of sentimental tears in her mouth. "Welcome home, Aunt Tess," she murmured, pressing a light kiss on Tess's pale cheek.

"Welcome home to you," Tess responded, then drew back to take Willa's face in her hands. "I want you to know how happy I am to have you home again—how proud I am of you."

Willa's gaze fled Tess's, then came back when the older woman gave her a tiny shake. "You've grown up to be just as lovely and capable a girl as I always thought you would."

Willa was too choked to speak, grateful when her aunt gave her another hug and she didn't have to.

"And now I'm afraid I do need that nap," Tess admitted as she released Willa and turned to head for her bedroom at the back of the house, leaving Willa in a backwash of emotion.

Not wanting to face Paige when she came in, Willa started toward the kitchen, but instead hurried into the den as the telephone began to ring.

"Did you get Tess settled in?" Clay's voice came over the line, his brisk tone making her stiffen a bit. At her quick answer, he went on, "I just wanted to let you know that Phil Spencer is here from Sheridan and he'll be available anytime after three for an interview and a look around the Circle H.''

Willa sensed then that Clay's all-business manner over the phone was because Phil Spencer was there with him. ''You can send him over anytime,'' she responded, hinting she wanted to conduct her part of the interview without Clay present. Clay had been able to arrange for Phil to come down for an interview quickly and Willa was hopeful that the man would be suitable so she could hire him and have him start managing the Circle H within the month. But, as per her agreement with Clay, she had final approval of the man, and if he didn't seem right for the job, she would simply not offer it to him.

Willa hung up the phone just as Paige came in, and she frowned at the unpleasant reminder that the interview and tour she'd planned for that afternoon might not be as private as she'd hoped.

PHIL SPENCER WAS a short, sturdily built man of forty whose likable personality enhanced his experience and qualifications. He impressed Willa as a good choice for a foreman. By the time she'd finished giving him a tour of the ranch—partly on horseback, mostly in the truck—she'd decided to hire him. Since she'd already read his letters of reference and discussed his resumé with him, she had only to talk salary and tell him the job was his if he wanted it. They were just getting settled in the den, when Paige came in.

''We haven't been introduced yet,'' Paige said, turning her best practiced smile on Phil, who seemed taken aback by both Paige's attention and her beauty.

''Phil, this is my cousin, Paige Harding,'' Willa said. ''Paige, Phil Spencer.'' With the introductions out of the way, Willa had every intention of getting rid of Paige. "Phil and I will be finished in here in just a few more minutes," she prompted, hoping Paige would take the hint and leave.

Paige took the hint all right, but instead of leaving, she perversely went over and seated herself behind the desk, her officious manner as she took up Phil's resumé and letters of reference making Willa cringe.

Willa tried again. "Phil and I still have some things to talk over, Paige. I think we'd both be more comfortable with a little privacy."

Paige glanced up and fixed Willa with an icy stare. "I'd like to interview Phil myself, if you don't mind," she said, then scanned the papers before her as if she knew what she was doing.

"Go ahead and have a seat, Phil," Willa invited as she gestured to one of the wing chairs in front of the desk, resigned to Paige's interference as she seated herself opposite him in the other chair. If Phil took the job, he'd likely be exposed to a lot of meddling from Paige and it was just as well to let him experience it firsthand before any agreements were reached.

"On the basis of this resumé and these recommendations, I'd say you're just the man I'm looking for," Paige remarked as she finally looked up. "How soon could you start?"

Willa shifted in her chair, irritated that Paige was usurping her authority. "Phil and I still have a few more things to discuss before either of us makes a final decision," Willa said, feeling embarrassed for herself and for Phil, who looked faintly uneasy.

"Discuss whatever it is you think you have to, Willa." Paige got to her feet and walked around the front of the desk to shake Phil's hand. "But as far as

I'm concerned, Mr. Spencer is our new foreman." Phil got up in a gesture of politeness to Paige, but Willa could tell he felt uncomfortable. "I look forward to having someone competent around to take care of things for Mother and me."

WILLA RODE the sorrel gelding to the top of the rise and reined him to a walk, giving him a chance to cool down and catch his breath. Feeling guilty for the hard, early evening ride, she reached down to pat the horse's damp neck, murmuring an apology as she scanned the network of corrals and ranch buildings of Orion in the distance.

She'd needed a hard ride after her latest no-win confrontation with Paige. She'd needed to dispel not only her ever increasing wariness of her cousin, but also the intense feeling of anger and frustration Paige provoked. That she'd also needed to see Clay again was something she didn't let herself dwell on.

Earlier, Paige had come to the den determined to go over the books—supposedly to familiarize herself with what was going on. In her usual frantic manner, she had dragged everything from the cabinet there, haphazardly strewing ledgers and papers about. She'd then demanded that Willa not only explain it all to her, but also account for every cent she'd spent so far—an accounting Paige had challenged and criticized at every turn. Easily recognizing Paige's sudden interest for the harassment it was, Willa had finally given up trying to appease her and had placed everything back in the cabinet before leaving the house.

Willa guided the sorrel toward the final gate from the pasture, leaning down to unlatch it before she rode through. Careful to secure the gate behind her, she urged the horse toward the lane that led to the back of the house.

"It's been a long time since I've seen you ride in like that," Clay remarked as he watched her dismount at the edge of the lawn and walk toward the patio. Willa glanced back the way she'd come, reminded that from where Clay sat in the lengthening shadows, he could have seen her the moment she'd ridden over the rise.

"It has been a while, yes," she answered softly.

Willa searched Clay's face as he sat on a cedar lounger with his feet up, his long, denim-clad legs stretched out and crossed casually at the ankles, his dark hair damp from a recent shower. With a lazy expression on his face and a cold beer in his hand, he was the picture of relaxation. Willa couldn't help but smile.

"You look like one of those beer commercial cowboys who kick back at the end of a hard day and do some recreational drinking."

"And you're a sight for sore eyes," he said huskily before he let his gaze roam leisurely downward. "Tell me, whatever happened to that little dress you wore to Angie's birthday party that time?"

Taken aback by the question, Willa flushed, knowing exactly which dress he was talking about. She shrugged a shoulder vaguely. "Aunt Tess probably threw it out. It disappeared from my closet shortly after the party."

Clay chuckled. "You were a mischief back then, Willa," he said, as if he were fond of the recollection. "Care for a cold one?" he offered as he tilted the bottle toward her. "I think I might even have some wine cooler."

Willa shook her head, a bit too unsure of Clay in his present mood. "Not now, thanks."

"Then come on over and sit down."

Willa nudged a padded cedar chair closer to Clay's lounger with the toe of her boot and sat down, tugging off her hat and leaning back, suddenly feeling relaxed. This is what it would be like, she mused, if she and Clay could be here together for the rest of their lives; the end of a workday could be this peaceful, this companionable.

"What's it been, a week?" Clay asked, breaking into her thoughts.

"A week for what?"

"Since we saw each other last," he clarified, reminding her that she'd not seen him since before her aunt had come home from the hospital. It had been two days since she'd met with and hired Phil Spencer, but she'd barely talked to Clay since then, what with the extra work she'd taken on trying to get the quarters at the bunkhouse ready for the new foreman.

Willa shook her head. "It's only been about four days."

Clay took a swig of his beer, his eyes on her all the while. "Have you been avoiding me?"

"I've been a little busy," she said, then added defensively, "I did call to tell you about hiring Phil Spencer."

"But you haven't returned any of my calls since then."

Willa's face showed her surprise. "Which calls were those?"

"I don't suppose Paige told you I stopped by yesterday, either," he said, his mouth twisting at the corners. "She said you were out checking cattle."

The anger and frustration she'd managed to forget about for a while came rushing back. "It must have slipped her mind, what with Tess home and all," Willa said as offhandedly as she could manage, doing her best to conceal her true feelings. Besides, criticizing her cousin to Clay would only make her look petty.

"I'd hate to have to get along on the kind of memory Paige seems to have," he commented. He took another sip of his beer before he spoke again. "You and Paige are still having serious problems getting along in the same house, aren't you?"

Willa's gaze streaked from his knowing expression. Surprised at the emotion that welled up at his perception, she looked down and toyed with the black leather band of her hat as she debated the wisdom of confiding in him.

"It won't be for much longer. Either she'll go back to New York or I'll be heading back to Colorado."

"I thought we talked about that," he reminded her, his voice going lower. "I thought you understood that I didn't want you to rush off."

Willa glanced up at the words, unable to help either the deep thrill of hope she felt or the sense of caution.

"I've got a couple of more weeks before Phil Spencer takes over," she pointed out. "That's not exactly rushing off."

Clay studied her a moment. "But when the two weeks are up, you'll be gone." It was a statement.

"I have a job to get back to," she said quietly, for the first time seeing her responsibility as an owner of the D & R as a burden.

"There are other jobs, Willa. You could find another one a lot closer to Cascade." The sternness in Clay's voice both surprised and delighted her. "If you're any good with horses at all, you could get on just about anywhere.''

"I'm happy doing what I do now," she said carefully, unable to quite bring herself to tell Clay about her ranch. If he pressed for her more, she'd tell him, but until then, she'd obey for a little longer the caution she felt.

"You don't think you could be happy doing the same job for someone else?" he challenged.

"I suppose it's possible." Willa felt relieved when the frown lines on Clay's face eased and he fell silent. Letting out a deep sigh, she started to relax, until she caught the disturbing glimmer in Clay's dark eyes.

"Two weeks isn't a lot of time."

The slow smile that slanted his mouth moved through her like an electric charge as he set his beer on the table nearby, then swung his feet over the side of the lounger to bring himself face to face with her.

Willa looked deep into his half-lidded gaze and felt her blood turn thick at the message she read there. "Time?" she asked, her voice breathless with tension as she responded to the look and issued a modest sensual dare. "For what?"

"For you and I to explore the feelings between us." Willa's breath caught as Clay reached out and enveloped her hand in the hard warmth of his before he stood and pulled her to her feet. "Come on inside with me, Willa."

She froze for a moment, unable to follow Clay inside to what she instinctively understood would bring them closer to sexual intimacy, yet not quite strong enough to flee the tumultuous mixture of fulfillment and complication such intimacy would bring into her life.

She tried to think of all the reasons she had for not going in with him, for not allowing anything deeper to happen between them, but the old feeling of betrayal simply wasn't as strong anymore. Gone, too, was her fear that some incident could again cast doubt on her word and destroy his trust. A sense of security she'd not thought she'd feel again sprang to life at the realization.

"Willa?" Clay's voice was coaxing as he gave her hand a gentle squeeze. "I knew a precocious little girl once who wasn't afraid of anything."

Willa's pulse quickened at the affection behind his words. "I think there's a lot more at stake here than that precocious child had the good sense to consider," she added.

One side of Clay's mouth slipped up a notch in approval. "I'm glad she's grown up enough now to realize it."

Willa's resistance melted dangerously as she searched Clay's tender expression. The love she'd always felt for him suddenly swelled her heart to the bursting point and she could no more have turned away from him and gone home than she could have stopped her own breathing. A feeling of inevitability stole sweetly over her and she walked with him to the sliding glass doors that led from the patio into the house.

"I'd better call down to Frank and have him see to your horse," he said once they were inside, and she waited as he stepped into the kitchen and made the call. It only took a moment, but to Willa it seemed much longer.

"All taken care of," he told her when he'd finished. "I'll have someone trailer your horse to the

Circle H tomorrow. You think you'd be interested in some supper?''

The relief she should have felt at his suggestion didn't materialize. Instead she was on edge, unaware of the restless look she gave him as she tossed her hat to a chair and tried to calm herself.

"Are you?" she asked, not wanting to admit that supper was the last thing on her mind.

"Not particularly," he replied as he started her way, then angled past her toward the modest bar nearby.

Willa was stunned by the sharp disappointment she felt because he had avoided touching her.

"Can I get you that wine cooler now?" he asked solicitously as he opened the liquor cabinet, then glanced back at her. "Unless you'd rather have a mixed drink." From the slight smile that pulled at his lips Willa knew he'd seen the quick flush that had come into her cheeks and that he'd correctly interpreted it.

"How about scotch?" she replied quietly, opting for something strong.

Clay's brows arched. "Don't tell me you're in need of a little false courage?" he chided as he selected a bottle and a stout glass.

Willa slid her hands into her jeans pockets to still their tremors and turned away to wander toward the huge stone fireplace that dominated the wall between the living room and the formal dining room on the other side. "Something like that."

Clay poured the drinks and passed Willa her scotch. Before she could taste the golden liquid, Clay held his glass up in a toasting gesture. "To us, Willa," he pronounced softly as their glasses touched.

Willa couldn't pull her eyes away from the smoky sensuality in Clay's dark gaze as she sipped her drink and watched him over the rim of her glass.

The jittery feeling of tension that had pulled her nerves too taut began to ease as the heat of the strong malt began to soothe away her nervousness.

"Better?" he asked after she'd had a second sip and lowered her drink to rest on the palm of her other hand.

"Much," she replied with a smile. Clay reached out and traced her jaw lightly, his gentle touch sending a flash of warmth through her.

"You aren't in any hurry to get home tonight, are you?" he asked, his dark eyes delving so deeply into hers that she had the startling sensation he could see into her very soul.

"No," she said, the word barely making a sound as it left her lips.

"That's good."

Willa's breath caught as Clay gently took her glass and set it next to his own on the mantel.

"'Cause you know something, Willa?" he asked as he took hold of her fingers and pulled her closer. "If you're only going to give me a couple of weeks to change your mind about moving north, I think I'd like to put this time to better use." His midnight-dark eyes kindled with the fire of intent as he placed her hands on his chest, then reached down to grip her waist.

Slowly he lowered his head and brushed her lips lightly with his own, his breath mingling with hers as he deliberately flirted with her mouth. "You know how much I care for you, don't you?" he rasped, his lips maintaining their feather light strokes as Willa's hands ventured upward. "I can't let you just run off," he whispered, his lips pressing a bit harder, clinging a bit more provocatively as Willa strained to get closer.

With each brush of his mouth, his breath became more ragged, its uneven cadence heightening Willa's excitement, until she was driven nearly wild with wanting.

Unable to bear another moment of his teasing, Willa speared her fingers into the thick hair above his collar, pulling him down as she rose on tiptoe and fused her lips to his. His response was instantaneous as he ground his body against hers, deepening the kiss until Willa lost track of everything but the primitive need she had for this man and the absolute compulsion she felt to give herself to him totally.

Clay's mouth moved off hers and glided to her ear. He took his time there before he pressed a series of light lingering kisses on the delicate spot just beneath it that robbed her body of strength. Before she realized what he was doing, he leaned down and hooked his arm behind her knees to lift her gently against his chest.

Faintly startled, Willa opened desire-weighted lashes to the burning lights that shone in his dark eyes. Understanding flickered between them and Willa made no sound of protest when Clay started for the hall that led to the master bedroom.

When he stopped at the edge of the bed, he lowered her to her feet, his mouth reclaiming hers for a fiery kiss that shocked and inflamed them both. When his lips finally released hers Willa could barely do more than cling to him.

With a slowness that served only to escalate the deep longing between them, Clay began at the open neckline of Willa's blouse, unfastening a button, then leaning down to kiss the bit of flushed skin he exposed before bringing his mouth up to graze leisurely over the silken skin of her neck. Steadily his hand moved downward, until Willa was forced to grip his shoulders tighter to keep her balance, so overwhelmed was she by the rippling tides of sensation that quaked through her.

"Willa?" Clay's voice was rough with emotion as he parted the facings of her blouse to gently caress her lace-clad breasts. Willa heard the unasked question and felt everything within her strain to answer as she opened her eyes and looked up at him.

This was the man she would love for the rest of her life. The feelings she'd had for him years ago had survived the very worst and had somehow been resurrected into something much more mature, something much deeper than fleeting infatuation. The love she felt for him was as vital to her as her own heartbeat, and if she couldn't do something to express it now—to in some way acknowledge it—she wasn't certain she'd be able to live with herself.

Still, there was more than a little fear inside her, fear that robbed her of words and made her drop her eyes from the passionate turbulence in his.

Unable to say what she felt or to verbalize her consent, she instead trailed her fingers over the muscle and sinewed lines of his wide shoulders and down his shirt front. The pearled snaps of his western shirt gave easily to her slow, deliberate little tugs, which exposed his hair-rough chest and lean middle, until she was able to pull his shirt from his waistband and slide it off. Her eyes crept up to his. She was thrillingly aware that his fingers were moving a bit more urgently on her and that his breathing was erratic.

Clay's eyes were black with passion and desire as he pushed her blouse back and drew her sleeves down her arms to fall to the floor. Willa felt the slight tremor of his fingers when they returned to the front of her bra and gently worked the catch to free her breasts. Her eyes drifted closed in ecstasy as the sweet abrasion of his calloused fingertips was followed shortly by the warmth of his mouth.

"I want you, Willa," he breathed against her, his voice gruff as she ran her hands over the sculpted flesh of his shoulders and back, reveling in the solid male feel of him.

Willa didn't realize Clay had guided her backward until her legs touched the side of the mattress. He lowered her to the bed, then followed her down, his lips reclaiming hers as he lay beside her and slid his hard thigh possessively over hers.

"I want you, too," she managed to whisper, barely remembering to substitute the word *want* for *love* when Clay's lips slid off hers to nibble their way down her neck to her breast. He had just begun to toy with one rosy crest, when the telephone beside the bed jangled.

Without hesitation, Clay reached over and flicked off the bell as he continued to lavish her with attention. Nearly oblivious to the slight interruption, Willa couldn't touch him enough, her hands combing through the lushness of his hair and tracing the grooved line of his spine as he teased her nearer the unknown.

Nothing in the world mattered to her except this man and the deep compelling need she had for him.

The chasm of emptiness deep within her was begging to be filled, and the more acutely she felt the need, the closer she sensed satisfaction was.

Clay had just lowered his hand to the snap of her jeans, when a loud hammering began at the other end of the house. Neither of them responded at first, so thick was the sensual haze that surrounded them. Only when the pounding began a second time did Clay show any interest in dealing with it. With a soft curse, he levered himself away from her and got up to grab his shirt, his dark eyes snapping with annoyance as he shrugged it on and hastily fastened it.

Willa slid to the edge of the bed and reached for her discarded blouse before she sat up and covered herself, her cheeks tinged with shy color.

"I won't be long," Clay promised as he leaned down, catching her chin and lifting her face for a swift hard kiss. "Wait for me?"

Willa nodded and watched him stride out as the urgent pounding began again. It was when she heard the low murmur of male voices that an uneasiness began to penetrate the sensual euphoria she was in. Sensing something was wrong, she quickly got dressed.

She had just stepped out into the hall, when she heard Clay coming through the house, the sound of his long swift strides sending a tremor of foreboding through her.

He slowed when he saw her, the grim set of his face softening at her worried expression. Willa felt her heart begin to thud with alarm as he crossed the distance between them and gently gripped her arms as if to steady her.

"It's Aunt Tess, isn't it?" she asked, the terror she felt sending a shaky weakness through her as she clutched his muscular forearms.

Clay's grip tightened and Willa's heart plummeted with dread. "Yes, honey," he said. "It's Tess."

CHAPTER TEN

"IT'S NOT AS BAD as you think, Willa," Clay assured her. "Tess had a little spell tonight, but—" he gave her a slight shake when he saw the tears spring to her eyes "—she's all right now. Frank said Paige just called to tell us that Doc Elliot was out to see Tess a while ago and that he says she's doing fine."

"I've got to get home," Willa said, unable to keep the anxious edge from her voice.

Clay nodded. "I'll take you."

The ride from Orion to the Circle H seemed unbearably long. Clay had no more than brought the pickup to a halt beside the house than Willa flung the door open to scramble out and hurry inside. Clay caught up with her just as she reached the back porch.

"Slow down," he ordered gruffly as he braced a hand on the porch door to keep her from opening it.

Willa gave the door a futile tug before she turned toward Clay, her eyes flashing with fear and anger. "Just what do you think you're doing?" she demanded.

"If you could get a good look at yourself, you'd know."

Clay's words penetrated her anxiety and Willa made a visible effort to relax as he dropped his hand from the door and gathered her stiff frame into his arms.

"You let yourself get upset too easily where Tess is concerned."

Willa bristled at the observation and pushed back slightly to give him a look of defiance. "I love my aunt. How could I not care about her?"

Clay shook his head. "Caring about her is one thing—getting yourself this stirred up is another. I told you Doc Elliot said she was all right. Besides, how much love and care are you going to show her if you charge in there after the fact and get her all excited again?"

Willa's eyes dropped to his chest and the rigidity went out of her as she accepted his reasoning. "You're right," she admitted softly, then shook her head. "But I just can't . . . lose her now." Willa released an impatient breath. "I know that sounds selfish."

Clay lifted his hand from her waist and used the back of his index finger to brush away the tear that had tracked down her cheek at the admission.

"Tess's going to live for a lot of years yet. Besides, worrying about it is only going to make those years miserable ones for you." Clay bent his head and touched his lips tenderly to hers, coaxing back a bit of the sensual closeness they'd shared earlier. "That's better," he pronounced as he drew away from the brief kiss and studied the more serene expression on her face. "I think you're ready to go in now."

He released her, then followed her into the house, his hand settling on the back of her waist in subtle support when Paige turned toward them from where she'd been standing at the kitchen counter.

"How could you just ride off and not let anyone know where you were going or when you'd be back?" Paige demanded in an angry tone, careful to keep her voice low. "Mother was certain you'd been thrown or that you'd been bitten by another snake."

Willa was instantly alarmed. Suddenly she regretted having ridden off without a word after her argument with Paige.

"Was that what upset her?" Willa asked, already knowing the answer.

"What do you think?" Paige tossed her dark mane of hair challengingly. "You're going to be the death of her yet."

"That's enough." Clay's voice was hard.

Paige was startled, but barely missed a beat as she daringly redirected her tirade toward Clay. "I can't believe you're defending her."

"And I can't believe you'd hold Willa responsible for this. You're way out of line, Paige."

Paige's cheeks reddened. "I'm not out of line. You just wait. She'll show her true colors one of these days. We'll see then how easily you and Mother find some way to excuse what she does."

Willa shivered at the dark glimmers of promise in Paige's eyes as she said the words, doing her best to quell the panic she felt when Paige's gaze shifted from Clay to her. She read plainly the fear-induced warning in Paige's eyes, and was shaken as she sensed more clearly than ever Paige's absolute determination to thwart her relationship with Clay.

"I think I'd like to see Tess now," Willa murmured as she stepped past Paige and escaped into the hallway. Not finding Tess in the living room, Willa hurried on down the hall to her aunt's bedroom.

Tess was sitting up on her bed, her head angled back to rest on the thick feather pillows between her and the headboard, her eyes closed, the family Bible open on her lap.

Unable to tell whether her aunt was awake or napping, Willa hesitated in the doorway, relieved to see the calm, even rise and fall of her aunt's chest.

Reluctant to disturb Tess's rest, Willa was about to back quietly away and leave when Tess spoke.

"Willa?" Tess's soft gray eyes opened and she turned her head toward her niece, a small tired smile on her face as she raised her hand to motion Willa closer. "Land sakes, child, what a look you're giving me." The tired smile broadened a bit. "But, then, I guess you're about as a big a worrier as I am."

Willa stopped at the edge of the bed, taking the hand Tess held toward her.

"How are you feeling, Aunt Tess?"

"A lot better now. Just a little tired," she said, then added, "sit with me awhile?"

"Of course." Willa sat down on the edge of the mattress, then began gently, "I'm sorry I just rode off earlier. I should have let you know where I was going."

Tess's brows drew together slightly as Willa went on, "I didn't mean to worry you."

"Worry me?" Tess asked, genuinely puzzled. "What makes you think I was worried?"

Willa's face showed her confusion. "I understood you'd got so concerned after I rode off and didn't come back that you started feeling ill again."

"Who told you that?"

Hesitant to name Paige, Willa managed to avoid answering. "That wasn't what upset you?"

Tess gave a short chuckle. "If I worried every time you got on a horse and rode off, they'd have to lock me up in a straitjacket. Sakes, girl, you spend most of your waking hours away from the house or on a horse. Why would I get upset this particular time?''

Willa searched her aunt's chiding expression, uncertain what to say. Paige had obviously engineered something here, but what? And Tess had suffered a spell of some sort this evening. If it hadn't been brought on by something Willa had done, how had it come about? The thought that her aunt had become ill for no reason was far more distressing to Willa than the thought that her illness might have been provoked by some worry or upset she'd caused.

A look of comprehension crossed Tess's face and she released a long, tired sigh and closed her eyes a moment. She murmured something soft that Willa didn't quite catch. "What was that?" Willa asked, and Tess opened her eyes and looked at her.

"Paige and I got into a little argument earlier and I was fool enough to let it bother me." Tess gave her hand a squeeze. "I hate it when Paige and I disagree." Her voice went soft as she added with gentle pride, "She's the best thing Cal and I ever accomplished together, you know."

Tess's words brought a pang to Willa, but she managed not to show it as her aunt continued.

"And you know how emotional I let myself get. Doc Elliot warned me about becoming so worked up, but I just haven't got the hang of controlling myself yet. It was no one's fault but mine and I don't want you to give it another thought, you hear?"

"All right," Willa said, able to relax as her sense of guilt eased.

"Now that we've settled that," Tess said as an impish twinkle came into her eyes, "maybe we ought to talk about just where it was you took off to so late."

Willa couldn't suppress a smile at the lively curiosity on Tess's face. "I rode over to Orion."

Tess's brows went up as she nodded. "You've been over there visiting Clay all this time?" she pressed.

Willa's cheeks colored. "Yes."

"Good. Are the two of you on as good terms these days as I think you are?"

"So far," Willa hedged.

Tess gave a decidedly unladylike snort. "Don't you dodge me on this one, Willa," she warned good-naturedly. "I can tell just by looking at you that you and Clay weren't talking ranching all that time."

The color in Willa's face deepened. "You're right about that."

Tess grinned, her earlier tiredness fading. "Are you in love with him?"

Willa didn't hesitate. "Yes."

Tess patted her hand, the gleeful look in her eyes making her seem years younger. "And does he love you?"

Willa's smile wavered a bit. "I hope," she said softly, her slight shrug communicating her uncertainty.

Tess leaned toward her and gave her a hug. "He feels a lot for you, honey, that's certain. And there's no question the two of you are suited to each other." She drew back and gave Willa a searching look. "I don't think I need to tell you how much I'd like to see the two of you together. I think the world would finally come right for you both."

If only it would, Willa thought. But no matter what happened between them now, Willa still needed Clay to see the truth about Angie's death. Although she'd been able to somehow set all that aside earlier, she knew now without a doubt that leaving the past so unresolved was potentially dangerous to their future relationship. The issue of trust was far too important to them both to allow it to be swept aside by physical desire.

"I hope you're right," she whispered.

Tess gave her another hug, then leaned back against the pillows. "Now that that's all settled, I think I might rest a little longer and read before I get ready for bed."

"Is there anything I can do for you or get for you?"

"Not a thing I can think of," Tess said with a firm shake of her head. "You just run along now and don't fret."

"All right, Aunt Tess." Willa stood up and started toward the door. "Good night."

"Good night, Willa."

Willa stepped out into the hall and eased the door partway closed, glancing toward her aunt one last time before she made her way back to the kitchen. To her relief, Clay was alone, his hip braced against the kitchen counter as he sipped a cup of coffee.

"How is she?"

"She seems fine...a little tired," Willa answered as she crossed the room and helped herself to a cup of fresh brew from the coffee maker on the counter next to where Clay was standing. "Where's Paige?"

"She took off in her car a few minutes ago."

Willa heard the smile in Clay's voice and turned toward him. "I take it she wasn't too pleased about something."

"Some*one* would be more like it," he said as he set his coffee cup aside and reached over to pull her into the circle of his arms.

"Ooops, watch the coffee," Willa cautioned as some of her coffee tippled over the side of the cup and dotted the front of Clay's shirt.

"It'd take a lot more than a little coffee to douse the fire I've got burning," he said huskily.

"Is that so?" Willa's gaze fell from his as she sipped her hot drink and tried to ignore the excitement that raced along her nerves as he pulled her against his hard thighs. If she and Clay had made love earlier, she would not have regretted it, but now that common sense had reasserted itself, she felt more cautious than ever. It didn't matter that she and Clay were becoming involved and that he had forgiven her for Angie's death; he still believed she was responsible for it.

Yet as much as she wanted to tell him everything, to make him finally see the truth, her aunt's possible reaction to it and her own sense of pride still made telling him outright impossible. Especially now that her aunt seemed unable to cope with upset of any kind, she realized grimly.

"Why don't you set that coffee out of the way, darlin'," he drawled, and waited a moment for her to place her cup on the counter behind him. Without giving her a chance to protest, he bent his head and seized her lips with a hunger that made confetti of her thoughts. When he finally broke off the kiss, they were both trembling.

"I don't suppose there's much chance of us taking up where we left off earlier, is there?" Clay asked, a wry, self-mocking twist to his mouth as he said the words.

Willa couldn't help but giggle at the look in spite of the frustrated longing that gripped her, too. "No," she answered, then sobered a bit.

"I'm still rushing this too much, aren't I?" he said, the gruffness in his voice making her feel warm and wonderfully safe with him. "I can see it in your eyes."

Willa's gaze dropped to his chest and she smoothed her fingers over his taut cotton shirt front. "I think there might be safer ways to explore our feelings for each other."

Clay took a deep breath and exhaled it slowly. "Safer maybe, but I can't shake the feeling that you're slipping through my fingers. It makes me impatient to do something about it, to make you mine." He lowered his head and sought her lips again, his breath coming in agitated gusts over her skin when he ended the kiss and struggled for control. Willa was no more in control than he as she leaned her weight against him, her body slow to recover from its love-induced languor.

"I think it would be a good idea if I headed on home," Clay said as he eased her away from him. "No telling what kind of spell your aunt would have if she came out to the kitchen a few minutes from now."

Willa walked with him to the porch door, disappointed in the light swift kiss he gave her before he stepped out into the night.

THE WEEK SPED BY QUICKLY as Willa worked to prepare the bunkhouse not only for Phil Spencer, but for the two ranch hands Clay had found for her. The future of the Circle H looked far brighter now than when she'd first returned, and Willa was more than pleased with the way things were going.

Clay stopped over nearly every day and they went out together almost every night, which never failed to distress her cousin. As a result, Paige had become withdrawn, the deep circles beneath her eyes a vivid indication of sleeplessness. Though Willa felt some amount of sympathy for Paige, she was far too busy and much too happy to allow her cousin's apprehension to daunt her.

The almost constant state of euphoria she was in because of her deepening relationship with Clay gave her a lightness of heart that had been alien to her these past five years. Though she would never quite achieve the untroubled high spirits of her adolescence, inside she felt almost as carefree.

Yet as the days rapidly advanced toward Phil Spencer's arrival, the sense of optimism and anticipation Willa awoke to each morning began to give way to the niggling reminder that Phil would soon be taking over the Circle H and that Clay and her aunt expected her to reach a decision about staying on. Neither of them knew about her part-ownership of the ranch in Colorado, and the longer Willa put off telling them about it, the harder she was finding it to do so.

It came to Willa several times that she should tell Clay about her partnership, but something had always held her back. Besides, the subject hadn't come up again, and in the past five years, Willa had developed a habit of not offering too much information about herself.

As far as Aunt Tess was concerned, Willa wasn't certain how she'd take the news, so she found herself putting it off again and again, reluctant to cause her aunt any hurt feelings until she was certain of her plans.

As it turned out, however, whatever sense of guilt Willa had felt about keeping so closemouthed about the D & R was swept suddenly away the day before Phil Spencer was to arrive.

Willa finished briskly rubbing down the sorrel once she'd unsaddled him, then turned him into his stall with his usual measure of grain and fresh water. A feeling of satisfaction settled over her as she walked through the barn toward the shade-dappled sunlight of midafternoon. Thanks to the loan of Clay's men, most of the repairs around the ranch had been made. And now that the bunkhouse was ready for the new hired men, Willa felt for once as if everything were caught up. From past experience on a working ranch, Willa knew such an achievement was rare and fleeting, but she allowed herself to enjoy how ever many moments of peace those accomplishments granted her.

A smile touched her lips as she walked toward the house and saw Clay's pickup parked beside her car. Though she hadn't expected him to stop over so early since they were planning to go out for dinner that night, she was glad to see him anytime. As often as they were together, Willa couldn't help craving more, and her relaxed stride quickened as she came up the walk to the back porch door and stepped into the kitchen to head for the living room.

Surprised to find no one there, Willa was just about to call out, when she heard voices coming from the den. Though she couldn't make out what was being

said, she could tell from the bitter tone of Paige's voice
that something was amiss.

A sense of foreboding wrapped coldly around her
heart as she approached the open door, deliberately
letting the sound of her booted feet on the carpeted
floorboards announce her arrival.

"Good. You're finally here." Paige's odd greeting
directed attention to Willa as she hesitated in the
doorway. Aunt Tess turned her head and glanced toward Willa from where she sat in one of the wing
chairs. A shadow of worry came into Willa's eyes as
she saw clearly the strain on her aunt's face, which
gave it a grayish tinge.

She walked farther into the room as Clay sat down
on the edge of the desk, his long legs stretched out in
front of him. Willa didn't need to see his stern expression to know that something was very wrong, or the
almost fearful look of nervous agitation on her cousin's face that warned her Paige was up to something.

"Well, now that you're finally here, I don't see any
reason to delay this." Paige's announcement ran like
sandpaper along Willa's nerves as Paige left her
mother's side and walked behind the desk. Willa's
brow furrowed slightly as Paige took the check ledger
for the ranch account from the cabinet. Willa didn't
realize the significance of Paige's action until she
flipped through the pages to a space well beyond the
spot where the checks were currently being written out.

Paige cleared her throat nervously, then took a
quick breath before she glanced first toward Willa,
then toward her mother. Since Clay's back was toward Paige, he didn't see the look, and so couldn't
have guessed at its meaning. Willa saw it clearly and
understood instantly what was coming.

"As we all know, Willa's been keeping the books and has had control of the Circle H bank accounts since she's been here."

Willa's frown deepened in irritation, but Paige hurried on. "I've been trying for days to get her to explain things for me, but she's always got some excuse or other, so I decided to have a look for myself. It was when I started going through the check ledger that I started to get suspicious."

All too aware of what her cousin was up to, Willa murmured a soft "Don't, Paige," as a sick feeling hit her stomach.

"Don't what?" came Paige's belligerent question, and Willa knew then there was no stopping her.

Willa's gaze flicked aside those few inches toward Clay, but his face revealed nothing. There was no look of softness in his stony expression, and Willa suddenly found herself unable to look him directly in the eye, fearful of what she might see.

"As you can see, Clay—" Paige came around the desk and passed him the ledger "—there are three checks written out for several hundred dollars toward the back—checks we probably wouldn't have found out about right away," she hastened to add. Paige looked up and glared triumphantly at Willa as Clay flipped through the pages. "And each one is made out to Willa."

The soft sound of dismay that came from Tess penetrated Willa's shock and she glanced worriedly toward her aunt. Tess's eyes were riveted on her daughter in disbelief, but Paige hurried on.

"I couldn't believe it myself," Paige said, pressing her advantage, "until I saw the bank statement Willa got today from the personal account she'd opened for herself in town.''

"Oh, Paige, no. You didn't go through Willa's mail!'' Tess's exclamation went ignored as Paige grabbed for the envelope addressed to Willa and withdrew the statement. By this time Clay had tossed the ledger onto the desk and come to his feet.

Paige thrust three deposit slips into his hand. "As you can see, Clay, the figures on the deposit slips match the amounts written out of the Circle H accounts to Willa. Everything is in her handwriting, both the checks she made out to herself and endorsed, and the deposit slips.'' Paige took a breath that was only slightly irregular, as she feigned disappointment. "As much as I hate to think Willa would do such a thing, it looks as if she's been helping herself to Mother's money. And since she knew she wouldn't be staying on much longer, she was clever enough to write out the checks to herself from the back of the ledger so we wouldn't find out for a while. It's possible she even thought Phil Spencer wouldn't question it when he did find them, since she's family and has been in charge of everything.

Paige's voice grew stronger, condemning. "But the fact is, Willa's taken money that doesn't belong to her. Add to that the fact that none of us knows for sure where she'll be going when she leaves here, and I think she thought she'd be able to get away with it.''

Willa was so stunned by Paige's accusation and the obvious trouble she'd gone to to concoct such an outlandish scheme that she was speechless. Her mind raced to figure out just how Paige had managed to arrange everything to make her look like a thief. Then she realized the scheme would have been simple enough for a child to pull off. Paige could have easily got hold of Willa's checkbook, easily forged her signature on the ranch checks, then used Willa's deposit slips to deposit the money into Willa's account at a branch bank. After all that, it would have been easier still to watch the mail for Willa's bank statement and arrange a confrontation. That Paige had grown desperate enough to do such a thing shocked her.

"I think you need to say something, Willa," Clay said.

Willa glanced over at him, snared a moment by the utter seriousness in his dark eyes, the deadly quiet about him. Did he believe she was capable of stealing from her aunt? Willa's attention jerked toward Tess at the soft moan of anguish she let out.

"Yes, Willa," Paige encouraged, seeing her mother's reaction and Willa's obvious concern over it. "What do you have to say for yourself? How could you do this to Mother? How could you violate her trust and steal from her?" She turned to Tess. "We should think about pressing charges, Mother."

Willa started to shake her head in vehement denial, when Tess's watery gray eyes came up to meet hers. The pleading look of misery on her aunt's face stopped Willa from the outraged protestation of innocence she'd been about to make. As Tess's face began to crumple, it came home to Willa in an instant just how much more traumatic it would be for her aunt if she insisted that Paige had engineered all this, rather than accept the blame herself. *"She's the best thing Cal and I ever accomplished together,"* Willa recalled her aunt's words.

"Willa?" Clay's stern voice prompted her to answer, but the words were lodged in her throat. Tess's life was more precious to her than her own reputation, and she was terrified that this trumped-up confrontation was too much for her aunt.

Why hadn't she gone back to Colorado days ago? Why had she let everything go on? Clearly Paige felt forced to do this in order to keep the truth about the accident from coming out. If Willa hadn't been so greedy and foolish about Clay and gone home when she should have, Paige wouldn't have done this. Now the door would be shut to Willa forever.

Tess was looking pale enough to faint and Paige rushed to her side to kneel by her chair.

Clay's voice brought Willa's attention back to him. "You aren't a thief, Willa, and you're no liar, either."

Willa's lips parted in surprise at the utter certainty in his dark eyes, then came together again as she glanced worriedly toward her aunt.

Which would be worse for Tess to endure? Willa asked herself frantically. Finding out that her much adored daughter was a calculating liar, or that her black sheep niece was also a thief? In those horrible moments, Willa had to decide. This could be her moment to challenge Paige, to refute everything and clear herself once and for all.

Willa started to speak, to defend herself with the truth—even to the extent of telling them all about the accident—but Tess bowed her head in shame and clenched a small shaky fist to her pale lips, effectively squelching any thought Willa might have had of telling the truth. Suddenly overwhelmed with fear for her aunt, she managed only with the utmost self-control not to run to Tess to try to hug away her distress.

Tears stung Willa's eyes as she made the only decision she felt she could make. Her voice was a choked rasp as she said, "I'm sorry, Aunt Tess. I-I'll stop in town and see that the money is transferred from my account back into yours."

Tess seemed to wilt even more at that, but Paige's arms came around her, muffling her mother's soft cry against her shoulder. Willa didn't chance a look at Clay. The fury she sensed emanating from him was enough. Unable to control the tears of despair and impotence she felt, Willa turned and hurried from the room, taking the stairs to her room two at a time.

She paced the room as if trying to escape the utter desolation that had settled over her. Then, unable to bear another moment, she dragged her suitcases from the closet and swiftly gathered her belongings. It would be impossible to live here now. From past experience she knew the condemnation she would suffer and knew that this time she would not be able to bear it in silence.

She could have Paige's outrageous claims proven wrong, she reminded herself wildly, but to do so would devastate her aunt. With shaking hands, she managed to cram everything into the cases, painfully aware that leaving the Circle H would mean leaving the two people she loved most in the world.

CHAPTER ELEVEN

WILLA PICKED OVER the breakfast of steak, eggs and blueberry muffins the cook had set in front of her ten minutes before, but she had no more appetite for this meal than she'd had for the others Ruth Miller had prepared this past week. As always, her thoughts were miles away as worry and anguish continued to knot her insides. Finally, for Ruth's sake and because she planned to put in another hard day, Willa managed to clear her plate, foregoing a second cup of coffee as she pushed away from the table.

"You're up a little early, aren't you?" Ivy called from the doorway, then made her way across the large square ranch kitchen to pour her own coffee.

"No earlier than usual," Willa replied as she started to rise from her chair. Deke and the other ranch hands would be in for breakfast soon, and Willa was reluctant for her presence to again subdue their normally boisterous good humor at mealtime.

As much as she'd tried to hide her depression, everyone at the ranch seemed to sense it from the day she'd got back from Wyoming. She was uncomfortable with the careful way everyone behaved around her now and she didn't much like to acknowledge that they all acted as if they were walking on eggshells when she was nearby. Everyone was going out of his way to be kind, but attempts to draw her back into the mainstream of the D & R were beginning to wear sorely on her nerves.

"Are you gonna to be workin' that black colt right away, or can you wait around long enough for me to eat so we can go over some business?"

Ivy sipped her coffee and waited for her partner to respond, seeing, not for the first time, the restlessness in Willa as she reluctantly nodded.

"Anything in particular?" Willa asked as casually as possible, though she was more than a little wary of Ivy's tone. Until now, Willa had managed to evade any real explanation to her friend about what had happened at the Circle H that had made her leave so suddenly. But knowing Ivy as well as she did, she could see by the determined glint in the woman's hazel eyes that she'd finally run out of patience and aimed to have some answers.

"Yes, as a matter of fact, there is," Ivy answered as her look became more determined, and Willa felt a kind of relief brush through her. Ivy was not only her partner, but her closest friend. Perhaps unburdening herself to Ivy would help lift her heartsick feelings and give her a more objective outlook. Willa was failing miserably to get a firm hold on those things alone, so maybe it was time to hear what Ivy had to say about it all.

"Then I guess I'll grab another cup of coffee and go on into the den."

Willa settled into the comfortably worn over-stuffed chair opposite the short sofa in the sitting area of the den. From the sounds coming from the kitchen on the other side of the wall, Deke and their three hired hands were just coming in, and Willa closed her eyes wearily.

She remembered reading someplace that depression was often anger turned inward. As she rolled the thought over in her mind, she admitted to herself that at least in her case it must be true.

How had she allowed Paige to do it to her again? She should have been more wary, more careful of Paige. Instead she'd either tried to avoid too much open conflict with her cousin or simply ignored her.

Also, she should have swallowed a little more pride and had it out with Clay about who'd been driving when Angie was killed, while Tess was still in the hospital. Because he, too, had been concerned about Tess's health; it wouldn't have been too hard to convince him to help her keep the truth from her aunt—provided he had believed her at last. Then again, he might not have been able to mask a changed attitude toward Paige, and Willa was certain a sudden shift in his hostility would have distressed her aunt whether she knew the reason or not.

Willa let out a tired sigh. Trying to protect Tess was a never ending worry. Clay had been right. Her anxiety over endangering her aunt's frail health was making her miserable. It had kept her silent when she should have stood up for herself; it had made her sacrifice her reputation and her happiness.

A strong image of Clay came into her mind and a sharp pang went through her heart. Because she'd wanted to spare her aunt the horrible shock of knowing her only child's true nature, she'd also sacrificed her future with Clay.

"You aren't a thief, Willa, *and you're no liar, either.*" She went over Clay's words in her mind as she had again and again since she'd left the Circle H. Had there been a spark of sudden comprehension in his dark eyes, or had it only been a figment of her own anguished hope? Could he have at last come to the realization that she'd not lied about the accident? Willa couldn't trust herself to decide for sure. With a heart that sank deeper in her chest, Willa reminded herself for the thousandth time that he might only have been encouraging her to tell the truth about the theft from the Circle H accounts.

Willa heard the scrape of chairs in the kitchen and the sound of the men heading out to work. She didn't bother to open her eyes when she heard Ivy come into the den and close the door firmly behind her.

"Okay, Willa," Ivy said sternly as she seated herself on the sofa and took a quick sip of her coffee, "time's up."

Willa opened her eyes and smiled weakly.

"Let's hear it."

Ivy's demand brooked no argument and Willa didn't even try as she slowly began to relate what had happened. Ivy interrupted her right away and prompted her to start much farther back than she'd intended—especially the part about Willa and Clay reconciling and what had been happening between them since. Then, as was Ivy's habit, she continued to interrupt Willa at frequent intervals to dig for more details.

When Willa was finally allowed to get to the finish, Ivy swore colorfully for a moment, then grew quiet, her brow wrinkling in thought.

"Paige sure managed to home in on your weak spot," she finally commented, then issued a gentle challenge. "Do you think you can stand never seein' Tess again and havin' everybody you know back there—especially Clay Cantrell—thinkin' the worst of you?''

Willa shook her head sadly. "No. And it's tearing me apart, I'm afraid."

Ivy leaned forward and patted Willa's hand encouragingly. "I think your Aunt Tess's got a lot more sand in her than you give her credit for. If it were me, I think I'd be more upset and hurt because I'd lost the company of my favorite niece than I would be to find out the truth."

"'Only' niece," Willa corrected quietly.

"All right then, *only* niece. But I don't care how many nieces she's got, don't you think that losing you again hasn't upset her and jeopardized her health?"

"I knew she would be upset either way, Ivy," Willa explained tiredly. "I just thought leaving and letting Paige win would be less an upset. You don't know how much she dotes on Paige."

"Sounds to me like Tess dotes on you just as much," Ivy persisted.

Willa shook her head. "I can't take the chance."

"Heck, you took a big chance, anyway, by tearin' off like that," Ivy pointed out irritably. "I'd be downright shamed if my niece thought I was that fragile." Ivy's voice softened in regret at her characteristic outburst as she let out a deep breath and leaned back on the sofa. "But I understand, Willa."

The room grew silent until Ivy spoke again. "What about that Clay Cantrell? You think he fell for Paige's story this time, too?"

"I hope he didn't."

"Anyone who knows you, Willa, knows you couldn't have stolen from your aunt," Ivy declared emphatically. "And if Clay Cantrell couldn't see through Paige this time, he's sure not worth much."

Willa lowered her face to rub her forehead. "I thought for a moment he could see what Paige was trying to do—I even thought he might have finally realized that Paige had lied about the accident, too. But when I took the blame about the missing money, he was so angry." Willa's voice faded to a whisper. "Even if he'd doubted Paige's claims and that phony evidence, I'm certain he believed her when I said that." Willa dropped her hand and raised tear-glazed eyes to her friend as her mouth moved into a crooked, self-mocking smile. "I've made my own bed, haven't I?"

"I reckon so," Ivy agreed, "but ol' Paige was standin' right there handin' you the sheets."

Willa had to chuckle at Ivy's humorous way of putting it. "Well, have you got any enlightening words of advice that I probably won't take?" she invited, trying to lighten her own dismal mood as well as give her friend the subtle assurance that she'd eventually pull through all this—despite the fact that she herself secretly doubted it.

"You know I'm just brimmin' with advice," Ivy said with a wry grin, then sobered. "Have you thought about givin' Paige a call or goin' back up there and tellin' her you'll give her just so much time to fess up and straighten everything out before you talk to Clay and your aunt and do it yourself?"

Willa's brow furrowed and she shook her head. "It would never work, Ivy. Paige would never tell the truth about the money or the accident—especially the accident. She already admitted to me that she couldn't have gone through what I did after Angie was killed. She felt desperate enough to do this to me, to keep everyone from finding out the truth because she couldn't face being an outcast." Willa suddenly felt sad for her insecure cousin, in spite of everything. "Paige has always had to have everyone's attention. She always had to be the belle of the ball."

Ivy snorted. "Don't tell me you feel sorry for her!"

"Just a little," Willa had to admit.

Ivy threw up her hands in exasperation and thrust herself back against the sofa. "You're so danged softhearted it's spread up to your head, girl. No wonder you can't think straight."

"Gee, thanks. You know how much I like compliments," Willa kidded, trying again for a little humor.

Ivy stared at her hard for a moment, then released a frustrated breath. "I'm sorry, Willa. I thought things would get straightened out for you. Before I read your uncle's obituary and got you thinkin' about goin' up to Wyoming, I was beginnin' to feel like you'd finally got over everything back there. If I'd known you were gonna to end up like this I'm not sure I ever would have mentioned it."

"Don't be sorry, Ivy. You did what any good friend would have done. It wasn't your fault I let everything get so far out of hand." Willa sat up straight in her chair and got to her feet, leaning toward the coffee table to pick up her empty cup. "And what's done is done," she said, forcing a sureness to the words, which she didn't really feel. "Hearts mend after a while, but work just keeps piling up," she added, effectively changing the subject. "And if that black colt doesn't pitch me in the corner of the corral again today, maybe I can get to some of it."

"You just watch yourself out there, Willa. This'll be only his second time with a rider, and he's purely full of vinegar. We didn't name him Jack-in-the-Box because he's so easygoin', you know," Ivy reminded her, then added, "and give some thought about headin' up to Denver with me for the show the end of the week. If you're bound and determined to leave things the way they are back in Wyoming, I think you need to go someplace and do somethin' different, have some excitement. I don't like the way you been workin' since you got back. A little fun'll lift your spirits some."

Willa glanced back at her friend and smiled, glad for the suggestion. "Sounds good to me," she said, then carried her cup to the kitchen on her way out to the barn.

"ALL RIGHT, HARDCASE, let's try it again," Willa murmured with a grim smile of determination as she picked herself up from the hard-packed dirt and reached again for the reins and a hank of Jack-in-the-Box's black mane. The colt had been almost as fractious this morning as the day before, and Willa mounted cautiously, trying to ignore the pain that shot through her hip as she swung her leg over and slid her boot securely into the stirrup.

"It's about time you learned which one of us is more stubborn," she crooned softly as her grip tightened on the reins and she prepared for the bunching of muscles that would signal another fit of bucking.

Instead the colt moved easily forward, seeming to accept her weight as he pranced around the outer edge of the steel-railed corral. Willa was not fooled. As was the colt's habit, just when she thought he was cooperating he seemed to enjoy leaping into the air, coming down with his front legs stiff and his hindquarters high for the jarring buck that had unseated her three times, two days in a row.

Though Willa didn't favor the method of encouraging a horse to buck and riding it to an exhausted standstill, she was starting to give it mild consideration as the aches and bruises on her body began to flare into muscle-cramping stiffness. It had been a while since she'd had so much trouble with a young horse, and she was trying to decide if it was because of some error she was making in his training or simply because the colt was a handful.

The next half hour went smoothly. Willa was pleased the colt was already beginning to take signals from the reins and the guiding pressure of her legs. She murmured words of praise and reassurance in a calm steady voice and gave the horse an occasional pat, finally feeling satisfied with his progress by the time she rode him through the corral gate and dismounted to lead him to the barn to unsaddle him.

But the moment she started for the barn and the colt wasn't claiming her close concentration, the melancholy she'd managed to escape for a couple of hours settled over her once more. She might never see Clay again, or her aunt, and the very thought dragged her heart down as she was reminded again of how much she'd felt compelled to give up to in order to protect Tess's frail health. Willa rubbed the sore spot on her hip as she tried to walk out the stiffness, grateful at least that the new aches were physical this time.

"You're damned good with a horse, Willa."

Willa jerked her head up at the words, startled as Clay Cantrell stepped out of the shadows just inside the barn.

She froze in her tracks, her heart twisting with love
and uncertainty at the sight of him. Tall and lean, his
dark eyes and part of his face shaded by the brim of
his black Stetson, Clay was an imposing male presence. His white shirt emphasized the width of his
shoulders and the depth of his tan, his lean hips and
long legs were encased in new denim. Willa couldn't
help the raw pain that pulsed in her heart as her
yearning for him grew acute. It seemed like forever
since she'd been held against that hard, strong body,
and the compulsion to run to him and throw herself
into his arms was overwhelming.

But Willa didn't move, couldn't speak, as she tried
to read his stern expression, terrified to see rejection
and hatred, but unable to keep from looking.

"It's too bad you aren't as good with people."

Willa's heart lurched sickly at his harsh tone,
plummeting lower, if that was possible. "H-how did
you find me?" she asked in a near whisper, doing her
best to recover from the fresh emotional blow that had
dashed her hopes once and for all.

"Your license plates were from Elbert County, and
I've been over at least half of it asking for you." Clay's
face still revealed nothing but sternness.

"Did Paige and Aunt Tess decide to press charges?"
she managed to get out, rallying at the stirring of anger
she felt. If Paige intended to go that far, she was in for
a fight.

"No charges," he answered gruffly.

Relieved, Willa gathered the colt's reins tighter.
"Then why are you here?"

"I'm after my own pound of flesh."

Willa paled at that, oblivious to the black colt who
nudged against her arm impatiently.

"But you'd better get that colt put up first." Clay stepped aside and Willa numbly led the horse past him, stopping just inside the barn to lift the stirrup and begin loosening the cinch. Clay stood behind her and she could feel his dark eyes on every move she made as she tried desperately to keep her hands from shaking.

That Clay was very, very angry was no secret, but what he was doing in Colorado was. In those tense moments that she quickly stripped the colt of the saddle and turned him into the nearest stall, Willa tried to guess what he'd meant about being here after his own pound of flesh.

Finished, Willa squared her slim shoulders against whatever he would say and turned toward him.

The instant she was facing him, she found herself caught in a steely embrace as his lips came down on hers with nerve-shattering force. Willa couldn't help that her arms were suddenly around his neck. She welcomed the near punishing pressure as if she were starving. His lips gentled, but he continued to plunder her mouth as if he couldn't get enough, and Willa was helpless to keep from allowing it, giving herself over totally to his demanding kiss.

For the next moments, their world diminished until there was only the two of them. Everything else flew from Willa's mind and her head spun as joy rocketed through her. He was here; this was real and right. He was hers and this kiss was the seal, the brand that seared them both.

Clay tore his lips from hers and held her even tighter as he pressed his lean jaw against her hair and mumbled raggedly, "How could you do it, Willa?"

Unable to reconcile his words with the powerful emotions that had just swept through them both, Willa went still, her heart barely slowing from its wild cadence as it began to thud in dismay.

"How could you just run away and not give me a chance?" Clay released her then just enough to grip her upper arms and keep her just inches away as he stared down at her bleakly. "Did you think I'd be fool enough to believe that damned crock of bull Paige cooked up?"

Willa couldn't speak as sadness welled up inside her. The hurt was vivid in the deep emerald of her eyes as she recalled the other time he'd believed Paige's story over hers.

Clay cursed softly and his grip tightened. "I wasn't out of my mind with shock and rage over a senseless death this time. If I hadn't been so crazy with grief over Angie I would have seen through Paige's lies five years ago." Clay's voice lowered to a choked gruffness. "I probably knew it on some level all along, but when I saw how Paige was setting you up about the theft—could see her in action—suddenly it all became clear."

Clay crushed her to him, pressing desperate kisses into her light hair. "My God, what we've made you go through, sweetheart. There aren't words enough to tell you how sorry I am."

Willa could hear the tears in his voice, and felt a flood of her own cascade down her face and dampen the front of his shirt as she pressed her cheek against his chest.

Over and over Clay repeated, "I'm so sorry, baby, so sorry."

Clay was shaking as badly as she was when he drew just enough away to lift her chin with the side of his finger. The lips he pressed to hers were infinitely tender.

"I should have believed you back then, Willa. I should have and I didn't." His face was full of regret. "I can't give you back those years and I can't take away all the pain you must have felt, but I'm hoping one day you'll be able to forgive me."

Willa had a hard time finding her voice, but when she did there was no hesitation over the words. "I already forgive you."

Clay kissed her again, then hugged her tightly, and Willa reveled in the love and security she felt in his arms.

"What about that pound of flesh you said you came for?" she asked as she remembered what he had said, totally unafraid now of what he might have meant.

Willa heard the catch in Clay's chest as he gave her a squeeze. "I wanted that because you didn't try to get everything about the accident straightened out with me when you first came back to Cascade, and because you let Paige get away with her lies a second time. The truth is, though, it's you who deserves to get your pound of flesh—from both me and Paige." Clay pulled back and looked down into her eyes. "I thought I'd go crazy when you just walked out and disappeared. I was afraid I'd never find you again." His lips twisted wryly. "Then that red-haired partner of yours gave me a good going-over up at the house."

Willa laughed at the picture of Ivy giving Clay a hard time, mildly surprised that he had managed to get past her. "What made her let you see me?" she asked curiously.

Clay's face was utterly serious. "I told her I was in love with you and that I intend to take you home to Orion to be my wife."

Willa searched his eyes intently. "Because you want to make things up to me?" she asked, her lips trembling a bit at the disheartening thought.

"Hell, no," he burst out before his voice once again gentled. "I want to marry you because that sixteen-year-old child I tried so hard not to fall for grew up to be the woman I'm going to love the rest of my life. You had me by the heart from the moment I saw you at Cal Harding's funeral—much as I tried to fight it," he admitted with a self-mocking twist of lips. "I'd already decided I was going to declare myself and ask you to marry me before you could leave Cascade again, but then Paige gummed up the works with that damned stunt." Clay's brow grew dark with anger at the mention of Paige.

"What's happened to Paige?" Willa asked, still a bit awed by everything he was saying. "Is Aunt Tess all right?"

"Tess's fine. Worried about you, but fine. She'd already guessed about the accident sometime ago, but kept hoping she was wrong because she couldn't quite face the idea that Paige could have lied about it. She went through a rough patch for a day or so after you left, but she's dealing with it well enough to get by. I don't suppose, though, that she'll start feeling better until she sees you again and knows for sure you're all right."

Willa was relieved at that news. "And Paige? What about her?"

Clay's face went a little rigid. "After you left the den, I told her flat out I knew she was lying and that I knew she'd lied when Angie died. She finally broke down and admitted everything. Afterward, Tess made it clear that she still loved Paige and that the door was always open, but that until Paige made things up with you, their relationship was going to be strained. Tess more or less insisted that Paige see a psychiatrist, and I hear Paige left for New York on Thursday.''

Willa was quiet a moment as she tried to absorb it all. ''How do you feel about that?'' she asked gently.

''How do I feel?'' Clay thought for a moment, then released a deep breath, weariness flashing over his face. ''I'm not sure I can forgive Paige for either Angie's death or the lies about you—but I think I'm in need of so much forgiveness myself that I don't have a leg to stand on.''

Willa saw clearly the uncertainty in Clay's eyes as he said the words, the silent plea for reassurance that made him seem oddly vulnerable. Her heart ached at the look.

''I love you, Clay,'' she said with simple earnestness. ''I said I've forgiven you and I mean it. I'm sick of letting the past hurt us.''

''Then . . . do you think there's a chance you'll ever agree to come back to Cascade and marry me?''

Willa searched Clay's face for an indication that his proposal of marriage was in any way a kind of penance, but instead saw the love and longing in his eyes that mirrored her own.

Clay appeared a bit nervous at her hesitance. ''You could keep your partnership in the D & R, if you want. I'm not opposed, although I'm going to miss you like hell every time you think you need to come south to check on business.''

A soft smile touched her lips. "Thank you for not expecting me to sell out. This ranch and my partnership with Ivy was all I had for a long time." Willa's hand went to his cheek. She loved him more than she ever thought possible.

"Well? Are you going to say yes and put me out of my misery?" he prompted gruffly. "Or are you going to send me back past that red-haired lady wrangler and let her make good on her threat to pepper my hide with buckshot?"

Willa laughed, not at all certain whether her quick-tempered friend was above such a deed or not. Clay's lips came down lightly on hers, capturing the laughter and enticing more of the sweet, carefree sound of it as he ran a tickling finger lightly up her side.

Between the giggles and the kisses, Willa at last managed to get out a breathless yes before Clay's mouth fused hotly to hers, securing forever the bond between them that nothing would ever break again.

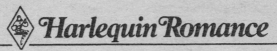

◆ Harlequin Romance

Coming Next Month

2935 TRUST IN LOVE Jeanne Allan
Fleeing from malicious, career-threatening rumors, successful model Kate returns to her small Nebraska hometown. There, unexpected help from onetime town rebel Ty Walker makes her stop running and fight back.

2936 PLAYING SAFE Claudia Jameson
Demetrius Knight disapproves of Grace Allinson—which suits her perfectly. After one heartbreak she has no desire to get involved again. Unfortunately his young sister's needs make it hard for Grace to befriend her while determinedly ignoring her brother!

2937 FEELINGS Margaret Mayo
Melissa, for good reasons, isn't interested in any man—much less someone like Benedict Burton, who demands that she scrap her adopted Miss Mouse appearance to be like the pretty, vivacious women he prefers!

2938 ONE-WOMAN MAN Sue Peters
Radio Deejay Berry Baker can't understand why her fund-raising plan for a children's ward at St. Luke's Hospital has turned into a contest for control—between herself and Julian Vyse, the senior medical consultant. But the battle lines are clearly drawn....

2939 MORNING GLORY Margaret Way
Someday young, talented Kit Lacey knows a man will come along to match her zest for life. And when Thorne Stratton, international news correspondent, arrives in Queensland's Eden Cove, he exactly fits the bill. Convincing him, Kit finds, is quite another matter.

2940 NEPTUNE'S DAUGHTER Anne Weale
Oliver Thornton is a name out of Laurian's past, and one she has every reason to hate. When Oliver turns up once more in her life, she's wary. Surely he will only break her heart—again!

Available in October wherever paperback books are sold, or through Harlequin Reader Service:

In the U.S.
901 Fuhrmann Blvd.
P.O. Box 1397
Buffalo, N.Y. 14240-1397

In Canada
P.O. Box 603
Fort Erie, Ontario
L2A 5X3

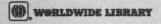

ATTRACTIVE, SPACE SAVING BOOK RACK

Display your most prized novels on this handsome and sturdy book rack. The hand-rubbed walnut finish will blend into your library decor with quiet elegance, providing a practical organizer for your favorite hard-or soft-covered books.

Only $9.95

Approximately 16" x 8" when assembled

Assembles in seconds!

To order, rush your name, address and zip code, along with a check or money order for $10.70* ($9.95 plus 75¢ postage and handling) payable to *Harlequin Reader Service*:

> Harlequin Reader Service
> Book Rack Offer
> 901 Fuhrmann Blvd.
> P.O. Box 1396
> Buffalo, NY 14269-1396
>
> *Offer not available in Canada.*

BKR-1A

*New York and Iowa residents add appropriate sales tax.